MW00945298

Bryan M. Powell

Million Dollar Murder

Books by Bryan M. Powell

Christian Fantasy Series

The Witch and the Wise Men
The Lost Medallion
The Last Magi
Journey to Edenstrae

The Jared Russell Series

Sisters of the Veil
Power Play
The Final Countdown

The Chase Newton Series

The Order
The Oath
The Outsider

Non-Fiction/Devotional

Seeing Jesus – A Three Dimensional Look at
Worship
Show Us the Father – A 30-Day Devotional
Faith, Family, and a Lot of hard Work – The
Grady Gillis Story

A boyish grin crept over Nate's face, and he shrugged his shoulders. For a moment, I saw the little boy inside a big man's body and wondered. She had him wrapped around her dainty finger and he didn't know it.

She flashed an award-winning smile in my direction. A contagious laugh percolated in her throat, and my heart skipped a beat. I too was mesmerized by her beauty. *She was only sixteen but looked much older and carried herself like her mother. I just hoped she isn't as conniving.* "It's nice to meet you, Lily. You look beautiful."

Lily's color, though highlighted by hours in the sun, darkened. She swept a wisp of honey colored hair from her shoulder revealing a dainty earring. Nervously, she gave it a slight tug.

"Thank you."

An awkward moment followed as I fought the urge to examine the plunging neckline of her dress. How a decent mother could allow her daughter to dress in such a provocative way escaped me. But then, Monica was no decent mother.

Where had the time gone? It didn't seem that long ago that Lily was a squirming infant wrapped in a pink blanket. Now she was a dazzling young lady. In an instant, my mind was transported back to a dark night. Though blurred by grief and confusing information, I saw another blanket.

It was blue.

And it was empty.

The moment quickly faded and I found myself standing in the midst of a crowd of strangers.

I had to stay focused.

It wasn't easy.

"Have a nice evening, Lily," I said as she pivoted and retreated back into the crowd.

For the next half hour, I attempted to get Lily off my mind. I was there for one purpose, to discover the connection between a rich land developer and Luciano Beretta. It didn't include lusting after my daughter, whom I had not seen in years, or fighting with my estranged wife.

Despite my caseload, I'd been able to fight off the aging process. My sandy brown hair had not thinned. And with only a slight greying at the temples, I felt I could pass as a younger man. So why have I spent the last two years of my life, since breaking up with Cami, sleeping in an empty apartment? Oh yeah, I was married to my job.

But Lady Justice makes a cold and fickle mistress.

As the evening wore on, I tried unsuccessfully to find a clique to break into. It was apparent everyone knew each other and were not interested in carrying on a conversation with a detective.

Hands in my pockets, I wandered from room to room in the palatial mansion. I counted scores of sculptured pillars and ornate fixtures. The one room I avoided was the lounge. Rather than being tempted to take a drink, I settled for the game room.

The ballgame playing on the big screen TV between two rival teams didn't hold my interest, so I excused myself. As I exited the room, I heard a collective sigh escape the lungs of those I'd left. Apparently, they were as uncomfortable with my presence as I was theirs.

Finding the solarium, I slipped inside and tried to relax and enjoy the wide variety of foliage. However, when I rounded one corner, I overheard two people speaking. The pattern of speech and angry tones told me to back off and listen. I couldn't help myself. I guess I'm an incurable snoop.

"What are you doing here?" one of the two male voices asked in a hushed tone.

"I had to come."

"Do you want to spend the rest of your life in jail?"

"No, but she's here, and I wanted to speak to her," came the whispered answer.

"You need to leave before someone sees you. Do you understand?"

Silence fell, and I wondered if the other person had left. Turning to leave, I heard someone speak one final time in a defiant, rebellious tone. "No, not until I see her." The loud rustle of shrubs told me the two had parted company—and not on friendly terms.

$$$

In the parlor, Carnes, the Butler, sounded the dinner gong.

The guests quickly moved to the formal dining room for a lavish banquet. While we dined, a string quartet played Bach and Brunner, Chopin, and Copland. The conversations were light, and without substance—the kind I loathed. That was until Nate Peterson and Mr.

Winager got into a heated argument over the freedom of speech issue.

Nate, the Public Defender, Ben Little, a city councilman and land developer, and Josh Silverman, a bank president, came out on the side of limited speech, while Harold Winager, a circuit judge, Edmond Yancy, Luciano's personal attorney, and Maurice Rivera, the financial wizard, weighed in on the side of open speech. The argument divided the guests nearly fifty-fifty until Luciano weighed in.

"Sirs, in my humble opinion in my home, you are at total liberty to say anything you please as long as it pleases me."

His statement seemed to settle the issue as the gathered assembly broke out in boisterous laughter.

Monica stood and tapped her crystal glass with the edge of her knife. Heads turned and the laughter subsided. "Ladies and gentlemen, may I offer a toast to our broad-minded and generous—I mean gracious—host, Luciano Beretta."

"To Luciano Beretta!" everyone cried. Following her example, they tipped their wine glasses and drank deeply.

As the conversations resumed, I couldn't help but notice Mr. Berretta. His face had reddened and the vessels in his neck bulged as he glared at Monica. *That toast wasn't a slip of the tongue*, I surmised.

Chapter Two

The dinner ended with coffee and dessert being served in the library.

I took a cup, filled it with the dark substance and sipped it. It was better than usual and I made a note to ask Luciano who was his coffee buyer. Taking another sip, I watched the crowd disperse and wondered what was next.

Luciano headed to the billiard room where he insisted the photographer take some pictures of Lily with a few of his cronies. Still others headed to the dance floor or to the game room where the ball game continued.

For a moment, I considered having my picture taken with Lily, but the restraining order Monica slapped me with years ago was still in effect. Reluctantly, I let the idea go.

Nate and Monica, dressed like Dracula's wife, made their way to the lounge and took a couple of seats at the bar. Feeling left out, I snagged a cup of coffee from a waiter and wandered down the hall. To my surprise, it was better than I'd expected. Over the years, I'd developed a taste for the exotic blends that most stores didn't carry.

As I approached the entrance to the lounge, I heard Monica's nagging voice. Curious, I held my position just out of sight and listened.

"I can't believe Luciano invited that scumbag Trace O'Reilly to Rafael's birthday party," Monica complained to Nate as they sat at the bar. Nate leaned heavily on his elbows. His head drooped, and his shoulders protruded upward. He looked like a vulture waiting for the next victim to die so he could gorge himself. Finishing one drink of brandy, Nate wiped his mouth with his sleeve and glanced at his wife.

"Yeah, well, Beretta knows what he's doing. If anyone can find a weakness in a person, he can. Once he gets his hooks into him, he will reel him in like a tuna. That's why he invited him."

Monica let out an exasperated sigh. "It doesn't make it any easier. Seeing Mr. Play-by-the-rules reminds me why I prefer bending them."

"Bending them?" Nate mocked. "You don't just bend them; you make them up as you go."

Monica straightened. "Shut up you jerk. You knew the score before you bought into this charade."

Nate opened his mouth but was cut off by the wave of her hand. Before he could recover, she turned and strutted toward the exit.

I ducked into a dark corner. *What did she mean by charade? Was this all a big setup for my benefit? I'll need to be very careful what I say around Luciano if he's looking for some leverage.*

$$$

Outside, the late October sky darkened into an angry caldron of swirling wind and rain.

Now I'm not a weather man, but I am smart enough to recognize a thunderstorm when I see one. The thick clouds I'd observed when I arrived had coalesced into a late autumn thunderstorm. Its gusting winds and icy rain chased the guests from the garden back into the mansion.

Ignoring the storm which threatened, I jammed my hands into my pants pockets and began to wander around. Listening, always listening. In my quest to shut down the drug trafficking trade in Sacramento County, I had to start somewhere. And with Luciano's ties to crime, though well hidden, he was a good place to start.

I heard a couple of men talking in the grand room and I stopped to listen while admiring the Mediterranean architecture. The conversation revolved around some innocuous topic, so I moved on, hoping they hadn't noticed me.

If I could connect Luciano with the drug trafficking in this state, I'd have it made, I told myself. Seeing Monica approaching, and not wanting to make a scene, I ducked into the art gallery before she found me. The small room housed Mr. Beretta's art collection. Among the many portraits, one captured my attention. It was the notorious portrait of "Madame X" by John Singer Sargent. As the wife of Pierre Gautreau, she was famous during the late 1800s in Parisian high society for her beauty and fabled dalliances.

The amateur art admirer in me caused me to slow down and appraise the piece more closely before moving on. By now, my feet reminded me why I longed for a desk job. After finishing my brief tour, I returned to the parlor. My bout with alcohol addiction and the subsequent recovery program limited where I could go. No more lounges or bars for me. As an alternative, I supplemented my yearning to have something in my hand by turning to coffee. Not just any coffee. I made it my business to learn everything there is to know about growing, roasting and refining the bean. Over time, I became a rather astute connoisseur of the brew. Along with becoming a coffee connoisseur, my conversion to Christianity was something of a pariah but that didn't bother me.

Looking around the spacious room, I observed a number of people sitting on plush couches. Large parlor palms and bamboo dividers separated the sitting areas giving the parlor a cozy, warm, inviting atmosphere. On one side of the room, I noticed an elderly woman. She was sitting in front of the fireplace observing the guests with a studied eye. Hoping to learn something from the wise old woman, I decided to join her. *Maybe I could relax and enjoy a decent conversation without feeling like I have to explain myself.*

On my way, however, I had to pass a cluster of men.

"Hey O'Reilly, how 'bout a drink?" one man said mockingly, holding out a glass.

I brushed him aside without comment and continued moving toward the woman.

"What, you're too good to have a friendly drink? I thought all Irishmen drank."

Heat clawed up my neck but I ignored the comment. All I needed to do was to cause a stir and that guard from outside would have plenty of reason to fulfill his promise and put a bullet in me.

Taking a seat across from the elderly woman, I smiled and waited for the inevitable question.

She studied me, appraisingly. "So you're the young man the city has its eyes on for the sergeant detective's gig," she said. Her shaky voice bore neither malice nor warmth.

I tried unsuccessfully to restrain a chuckle. "You're not one to mince words, are you. Mrs.?"

"Beretta. Ms. Rose Beretta, to be more accurate. I've never had much tolerance for spinelessness—not in myself, and certainly not in others." The dark pupils of her eyes bore holes through me, and I shifted uncomfortably.

"My late husband—God rest his soul—was one of those." She pointed her forehead toward a cluster of men dressed as turn-of-the-century gangsters. "He thought the way to get ahead was to make the right connections with just the right people and climb the corporate ladder by stepping on the little guy."

My eyes followed her gaze, and then looked back at her.

"Is that what you believe, Mr. Smarty-Pants detective?"

I was not used to being on the receiving end of an inquisition and I wondered if I'd chosen my conversation partner wisely.

The cluster of men broke into laughter, stealing the moment, giving me a chance to formulate an answer.

"No ma'am. I believe in treating everyone as I'd like to be treated—fair and square."

She harrumphed. "Sounds like the golden rule ... only around here, those with the gold rule. Don't forget, that's my son over there. He's just like his daddy ... always looking for an angle. If you let your guard down for one second, he'll seize upon it and reel you in like a fish."

My estimation of the woman rose exponentially. "Yes, ma'am. I'll keep that in mind."

"And another thing, Mr. Detective, see those women?" She nodded in the direction of a gaggle of provocatively dressed women standing too close to Rafael. "None of them can be trusted as far as you can toss them."

I smiled and gazed into the fire. "Besides yourself, is there anyone here that meets your approval?"

She paused and took a sip of her drink, swallowed, then cleared her throat. "Yes ... perhaps there's one. I've been watching people all evening. Seems like that's all I do these days ... watch people. But there is one who gives me hope."

My interest piqued and I scanned the parlor.

"Over there," she nodded. "There's a young girl. You met her earlier. She's got spunk and backbone. I think she'll go far in this world."

I followed her gaze until it landed on Lily. Pride crawled up into my throat making it difficult to speak.

"She's your daughter, isn't she?"

The observation struck me like a bolt of lightning. I felt my face heat as the elderly woman nodded knowingly. Without thinking, I pulled both my overcoat and sports coat off and laid them beside me.

"I thought as much. She's the spittin' image of you … in more ways than one."

I couldn't help smiling at her observation. "Guilty as charged; but I haven't seen her since … well, it's complicated. Her mother has done a good job of shielding her from me. As far as she is concerned, I don't even exist. And with my busy schedule and her mother's stubbornness, I'll be lucky to see her on her twenty-first birthday."

Ms. Beretta remained silent as an attendant added another log to the fire. He paused a moment, then glanced at my overcoat.

"Sir, may I hang this up? He asked, lifting it and preparing to take it to the cloak room.

"No, I think I'll hang on to it, but thank you anyway."

The man bowed slightly and laid it down. For a moment, he scanned the room as if watching for someone. I sensed purpose in his movements, but chalked it up to being part of his job … to see to the needs of the guests.

"Storm's getting worse," Ms. Beretta said, drawing my attention back to her. She glared at my shirt bespeckled with blood stains. "How'd you get the blood on your sleeve?"

Looking down, I pushed out a breath. "Stupid me, I was playing golf earlier and lost an expensive ball. I went into the rough to find it and got scratched up for my trouble."

She nodded, then lowered her voice. Her eyes glowed like two coals. "That's your weakness." She raised a bony finger and pointed at me as if she held a gun.

"You're willing to do anything to get what you want. That spells greed and trouble. Either way, if Luciano finds out about it, your goose is cooked. If I were you, I'd leave now ... before he reels you in."

Her observation fit me to a tee but that didn't keep it from stinging.

A clap of thunder cracked overhead, causing the lights to flicker and making the guests jump.

"It doesn't look like anyone's going anywhere tonight," I said, changing the subject and pulling on my sports coat.

"Young man, let me give you a piece of advice. Sleep alone. Keep your door locked. Don't go out for a midnight smoke, and whatever you do ... don't respond if you hear someone scream."

Her cryptic counsel sent an icy chill down my spine. I stood and looked down at her. Rose remained motionless, staring into the fire as if in a trance. I nodded silently and left her presence. Haunted by her warning ...

Chapter Three

❝Ladies and gentlemen."

Luciano's voiced bellowed as a new round of thunder rolled overhead. "I regret to inform you. The power is out, and we are running on a back-up generator system." He paused as a rustle of murmured complaints swirled like windblown leaves. "Plus," he continued, "moments ago, I was informed that the bridge at the bottom of the ravine has been flooded. It seems unlikely that anyone will be leaving this evening but no worries. We have plenty of room, and you are all welcome to stay the night."

A bevy of questions flew at him like a flock of quail. He silenced his guests with the wave of his hand. "Yes, my friends, you are quite safe here, and we will get you on your way in the morning as soon as breakfast is over, that is if Mother Nature cooperates. According to the weather service, it doesn't look good for the immediate future."

A few low conversations broke out among the assembled. Luciano clapped his hands, and a new round of food and drinks emerged from the kitchen borne by waiters eager to serve.

I glanced toward the place where I'd been sitting and noticed the seat across from me was empty. *Clever girl.*

Rather than let myself be tempted to take a drink, I pushed through the crowd and headed to the men's room. The conversation I'd had with Rose left my face burning and I wasn't sure if it was from the fire or her observations. As I turned a corner, I nearly ran into Monica … again.

"Stay away from my daughter," she demanded.

Dumbfounded, I raised my hands as she pressed closer. "I, I—"

She cut me off. "I saw you talking to her. You keep your distance or I swear—."

"She's my daughter too," I shot back, the memories of our bitter divorce still fresh on my mind. "I should have visitation rights like everyone else."

Monica glared at me. "And what's that supposed to mean?" jutting out her chin.

"Only that in the fourteen years since our divorce, I haven't seen Lily once. Other divorcees get visitation rights. So why shouldn't I?"

"Yeah well, other divorcees aren't drunks and stalkers. And if that sorry doctor hadn't botched the tubal ligation, we wouldn't even be having this discussion."

I was stunned at her admission. "You mean to say, you never wanted our—"

"Keep your voice down, stupid!" she spat, hurling words at me like fiery darts. "If you come near Lily again, I'll find a way to ruin your career. I swear."

I knew Monica's threat wasn't idle. I had already been written up for a DUI, and for drinking on the job. My recent conversion was seen by many as a ploy to get my bosses to back off. It wasn't working. Suddenly, I felt an old familiar friend creeping up my spine and fought the urge to lash out at Monica. I relaxed my clenched fists and took a deep breath. *Lord, I need your grace right now, or I might do something I'll regret.*

A triumphant smile tugged at the corners of Monica's lips. She knew she'd won … again. Her slender hand came up to her throat, and she began to play with a small key which dangled from a golden necklace. "Now get out of my way."

My face superheated. I stepped aside and watched her strut away. The sound of her high heels on the terrazzo floor declared she was a woman on a mission.

Turning, I continued my trek to the men's room, but as I passed a door, I heard it easing shut. *Was someone eavesdropping on our conversation?* I wondered. I shook the thought from my mind and stepped into the men's room. After soaking a hand towel with cold water, I applied it to my face hoping to cool it down. *What have I gotten myself into? I came here hoping to dig up some dirt on Luciano and all I got for my trouble was an ugly scene with my ex-wife. On the other hand, I got to see Lily up close. That was something.* After chiding myself, I cupped my hands under the spigot, filled them with water and slurped. After rinsing my mouth, I dried my hands and rejoined the party.

"Some party," I harrumphed.

Chapter Four

"Rafael, there you are, I've been looking all over for you."

Monica's smooth tones didn't allay his concerns. "Yes, Mrs. Peterson. What can I do for you?"

She edged closer to him, wrapped her arm through his, and played with a loose button on his blazer as she guided him to the solarium. Once she was sure they were alone, Monica turned her plaintive eyes upward and patted Sanchez on the lapel.

"Now Rafael, why so glum?" Holding her fingers slightly apart, she continued, "I have just a teensy addendum to my earlier proposition."

Sanchez shifted his weight, clearly annoyed. His hands clutched and opened as if they yearned to wrap themselves around her pretty little neck and squeeze. Her personal quest into his clandestine relationship with Luciano Beretta had paid big dividends. She was already milking him for a million dollars. It was bad enough to have Trace O'Reilly closing in on the Beretta crime-ring. He couldn't afford to have Monica blow the lid on his ties to a known drug-dealer. If word got out, Sanchez knew his chances at a run for the state's highest office would go up in smoke … and may even land him in prison for a long time. His only hope was that Luciano would sink Trace O'Reilly's ship first.

Sanchez took a hard swallow. "So, what is this teensy addendum?"

Monica lifted his tie and twirled it in her fingers and moved in for the kill. "I was thinking Chief of Staff would look good on my résumé. Don't you?"

Rafael's eyes bulged. "Chief of Staff?" he bellowed.

"Shush," she said, finger to her lips. "You want the whole party to hear your big announcement before you fire what's-his-name?"

"His name is Terry Parks, and he's very good at his job."

Monica straightened and looked the rich land developer in the eyes. "Good, then he won't have a hard time finding another job. Now when do you want me to start?"

Sanchez let out a string of expletives. "I'll tell him on Monday. In the meantime, keep your trap shut. I don't want the search committee to get wind of this until after my nomination is confirmed."

"Good … then your secret is safe with me." Lifting her fingers to her lips, she feigned locking them and tossing away the key.

$$$

Luciano lifted his head and peered over his glasses as Rafael stormed into the men's den.

Like a raging bull, Sanchez pushed through the blue haze of pipe and cigar smoke and leaned heavily on the edge of the pool table.

"What is it?" Luciano asked after eyeing him a minute.

"It's that woman," Sanchez said with a curse. "She's driving me nuts."

"You got a problem with a woman? Do as I do. Slip her a mickey and dump her in about a thousand feet of salt water."

Sanchez lifted his head. "Tell me I didn't hear that."

"Say what? Oh, I'm just kidding," Luciano said, slapping him on the back.

"I'm afraid it's not that easy. You know that witch Monica Peterson?"

"Yes, what about her?"

"She's got me by the throat. I'm already paying her to keep quiet about the Santa Vern deal. Now she wants the Chief of Staff gig."

Luciano inhaled and let it out slowly. "Don't tell me she discovered you swindled me out of the Santa Vern property?"

"It was a fair deal. I'm just a better poker player than you are," Sanchez huffed. "No thanks to you for setting me up with her in the first place. I wouldn't be in this mess."

"Well, it serves you right … How much is she into you for?"

Sanchez shrugged. "A million dollars."

"A million this year, a million next year, when will it end?" Luciano said. "She should be working for me."

"I thought she did."

Luciano held his stare for a long minute.

Turning, the wealthy land developer began to pace the floor, his patent leather shoes squeaking with every tread. "She's got to be stopped, but I don't know how. Oh, and by the way. Did you notice what she has around her pretty little neck?"

Before answering, Luciano pulled a fresh cigar from a wooden humidor and offered one to his old friend. Sanchez took it with a nod. "Yes. It is the necklace. No doubt the one with a certain key dangling on the end of it."

"Do you think she knows?"

Luciano shook his head. "I doubt it. But she may be getting suspicious. I could solve your problem, tonight."

"No!" Sanchez boomed. He was losing control, he could feel it. Over the years he'd been able to mask his symptoms, to control his urges, but this problem was getting out of hand. "Not with that hot-shot detective lurking around here. Why did you invite him in the first place?"

Luciano let out a husky laugh and lit his cigar. He took a full drag and exhaled. The smoke ascended in ever-widening circles. "I'm fishing. I thought I might need a man on the inside of the detective department and who better?"

"Well, whatever you do, don't involve me, and don't do it before my nomination."

Luciano whirled around and faced Sanchez. The veins of his neck bulged and his eyes burned like embers. "Look, Rafael," his voice rising above the din. "Who are you to tell me what to do? Remember, we're in this together." He slammed a fat hand down on the pool table so hard the 8-ball jumped into the corner pocket, then he stalked from the room.

Chapter Five

The howling wind and relentless rain pounded the stately mansion with a vengeance, yet its thick walls fought back courageously.

As the evening wore on, several of the worried guests paired off and headed to the guest rooms on the second floor.

After splashing my face with water, I reentered the parlor. Passing the butler, I gave him a slight nod. He regarded me with interest. I got the distinct impression he wanted to speak to me when Monica interrupted him.

"Keep your distance, old man and remember, you're just the butler," she spat out the last word with disdain.

"I was just helping Lily retrieve her earring," his voice barely above a whisper, but I heard him, nonetheless.

She pierced him with those malevolent eyes of hers. "You have no right, stay away from her or I swear ..." A round of laughter from a gathering of men drowned out the rest of what she said but I knew from personal experience, Monica never made an idle threat.

Carnes stepped back, gave us both a curt bow and receded into the background. As he turned, however, I caught a slight tremor on his lips and his eyes ringed with moisture.

Funny how you notice things like that.

With a triumphant huff, Monica whipped around and stomped away. Relieved it wasn't on me she was pouring out her vitriol, I took a seat in front of the fireplace. Extending my hands to the radiant heat, I tried to clear my mind. It didn't work. Monica's words haunted me. A piece of charcoal popped sending sparks up the chimney, and I pulled back. A woman's cologne wafted in my direction, arresting my thoughts. I dragged my eyes from the fire and caught a glimpse of Cami peering down at me.

"Whatever you want, I'm not interested." The words came out coarse. I didn't mean to sound so, so disinterested.

Cami's face darkened. "Why Trace, you couldn't mean that."

I didn't. I'd met Cami ten years after my divorce from Monica. It took me that long to get over her. Our two year fling was just that … a fling. It ended badly and I regretted it ever since. The thought of getting back together after two years was just too painful. I couldn't stand the risk of rejection, but my male pride had been wounded and I was still licking my wounds.

It occurred to me, the luck of the Irish didn't extend to me when it came to women.

Not at all.

Keeping my eyes from wandering, I tried to focus on the two cool blue orbs staring back at me. They showed no interest in me, at least not the way they had in the past. "Are you here to enjoy the fire and a few moments of quiet reflection?" I asked, trying not to sound too hurt, even though I was.

She took a seat next to me and squirmed. Lowering her voice, she said, "Actually no." The mint she had popped into her mouth failed to mask the alcohol on her breath. I pulled back and took a gulp of fresh air.

"It's your wife, uh, ex-wife."

"Monica?" I tried to hide my angst at hearing her name. Before tonight, I hadn't thought of my ex, but seeing her and Lily stirred up a cauldron of emotions I'd kept buried for years. "What's she up to now?"

Another ember popped sending a spark out upon the carpet. I tapped it lightly with my shoe and looked up.

"She's up to no good. That's all."

I smirked, "What's new? Why do you think she left me?"

Cami's raised eyebrows told me I'd piqued her interest. "She left you? That's not the story I got—the one she's been spreading."

I shook my head knowingly. "I'm not surprised. Ever since that last big drug bust, my name has become a household word. She's probably upset that I'm still around. Fact of the matter is, the way I was living back then, I deserved leaving, but that didn't justify her infidelity."

The ticking of the grandfather clock marked the moments as Cami stared into the fire. After a long pause, she continued, "This time I think she's really gone and done it."

"Why tell me?" I asked, my eyes searching hers.

"You're the detective. I thought you could talk to her, get her to change her mind."

"And when did you think she ever listened to me? What's she done now?"

She glanced cautiously around the room. After a beat she spoke, and then in a whispered tone. "Blackmail." The word rolled off her tongue like it was a curse.

Our eyes locked. I tried to imagine who or what she meant. "Blackmail? What are you talking about?"

"Monica came to me a few minutes ago and told me some tale of her having a special *arrangement* with Rafael Sanchez. That he'd paid her one million dollars to keep her trap shut about him and Mr. Beretta."

I stood and paced over to the large window to think. Suddenly, a bolt of lightning lit up the sky. One jagged finger struck a lone alpine setting it ablaze. Conversations around the room ceased as a number of shaken guests moved to the windows to watch the spectacle.

Cami joined me, unmoved by the sight. Her voice became cold as ice. "Plus, Sanchez is going to promote her to Chief of Staff in his political campaign. I've been with him a lot longer than that gold-digger. I should be the one he chose, not her." Her words sailed through the air with pin-point accuracy. "I won't let her get away with it."

"Look Cami, I know you've been working with Sanchez ever since you graduated from college. You deserve that position but this is just hearsay," I said, unconvincingly. "Not to mention it's been mingled with a bit too much alcohol. Why don't you hold back on this information until morning, and if it's still an issue, then, I'll look into it. How's that sound?"

Cami rubbed some wrinkles from her outfit. "I know what I heard, and a night in Beretta's lair won't change a thing." She turned abruptly and marched off.

I let a few minutes pass before returning to my seat in front of the fire. Its glowing embers reminded me of a demonic creature waiting to be stirred. Sighing deeply, I stood and headed upstairs. I found my assigned room, turned the knob, flicked on the light, and entered. Per Rose's instructions, I locked the door and slid the dead-bolt.

Chapter Six

The moment Trace left the sitting area, a shadow moved.

Seething from what he'd heard, Nate, who'd been sitting on the other side of a large parlor palm, stood and stormed from the room.

"That back-stabbing little snit," he muttered to himself. "If Monica thinks for one minute she's going to ruin my brother's chance at freedom, she's got another thing coming. I don't care if he fouled up, it happens. Sometimes people make mistakes, even doctors. Why she brought a malpractice suit against him after all these years, I'll never know. But I promised Nelson I'd do my best to get his case resolved, and I'm not going to let Monica screw it all up—not even for a million bucks." He stood and marched to the game room. He needed to cool off with a tall icy cold beer.

$$$

Lily caught Cami's attention. "Have you seen my mom?"

Cami paused and turned to face her. "Yes, she's around here somewhere. The last time I saw her, she was heading upstairs … but that was about an hour ago."

Giving her a shrug, Lily turned to leave. "Well, it is past my bedtime, and this storm doesn't seem to be letting up. I think I'll turn in. If you see my mom or my step-dad, tell them I've gone to bed and not to wake me until around noon."

Cami gave Lily a light hug. "Yeah, it's getting late." She paused and scanned the room. "And all these guys want to talk about is guns, girls, or games ... and not particularly in that order. I've had it with them. I'll turn in soon, but first I need to get the key to my room." She sauntered to the lounge to get her room assignment. Seeing a couple of friends, she perched a hip on a stool and joined the gossip.

$$$

Lily stepped out of Cami's space and watched her move away.

She barely knew the woman, yet in some strange way felt a kindred spirit with her. The few brief encounters they'd shared were precipitated by her mom's proximity to Mr. Sanchez. He seemed to be the common denominator in everything in her life.

Not wanting to dwell on the kind of relationship her mom had with the powerful land developer, she headed to her room. She paused at the foot of the stairs and caught her breath. A wave of nausea swept over her. Clutching her stomach, she wished Luciano had an elevator, but she was young. So why was she always tired?

Recently, she'd been experiencing severe pain in her abdomen coupled with blurred vision. She'd chalked it up to the usual stuff women experience. Looking up, she glimpsed her mother, who was standing at the top of the steps looking down. Their eyes met and for a moment Monica's smile stayed in place. But as a man carrying an armload of clean towels stepped around her, Monica's smile faded.

Without so much as an 'Excuse me,' the man began to climb the stairs. Letting out a frustrated breath, Lily considered upbraiding him but felt too ill for a confrontation.

Chapter Seven

I had not been in my room for more than ten minutes before the grandfather clock at the bottom of the stairs faithfully marked the passage of time.

With majestic tones which resounded throughout the mansion, it sounded out its message on the quarters and halves. I glanced at my watch. *Eleven o'clock, right on time.*

Sitting on the edge of the bed, I contemplated the words of Mrs. Beretta. After many wasted years, it seemed my life was finally coming together ... maybe for the first time.

Even before my divorce, my job and my drinking consumed me. But later, after my break-up with Cami, I met Ron Wolverton. He led an alcohol and drug recovery ministry at a local church, and my life hadn't been the same. It was Ron's tough love that showed me God wasn't looking for religious do-it-yourselfers. He was looking for broken and repentant people who He could redeem, repair, and heal.

I still remembered the deep peace which came over me the night I asked Jesus into my broken life. I only wished I'd done it much sooner. Besides fathering Lily, my salvation had been the best thing that had come out of that situation.

As rotten to the core as she was, I couldn't believe Monica would stoop to blackmail. That was a serious matter. Shaking off the worries, I pulled a small Bible from my coat pocket and began to read my favorite passage in Psalms. I lost track of time as I meditated on the verses before me. As I concluded my evening routine, voices in the hallway interrupted my thoughts. First, there was a man's voice ... his tone, rough, demanding. But the longer I listened to the man and woman argue, the more convinced I became there were more than just the two of them. A younger woman's voice added to the confusion. Resisting the temptation to open the door, I crept closer and leaned against it ... listening.

The argument continued.

Against my better judgment and Rose Beretta's warning, I slid the deadbolt back, twisted the knob and eased the door slightly open. By now, I'd heard enough of the conversation to pique my interest. One of the women thought the other was prying into her affairs and warned her to back off.

Heart pounding in my ears, I quietly stepped into the hall. The generator had been switched on and the emergency lights cast the figures around the corner in eerie shadows. My nose immediately told me what my ears had missed. Monica's signature cologne hung thick in the air. With a quick step, I crept closer to the corner.

"Give it to me, now!" It was definitely a man's voice.

"Yeah, you should return it before you get in trouble," the lighter female voice demanded.

"Stay out of this. It's none of your business," the other woman's words were clipped.

"None of my…"

"Hold your voice down. You want someone to hear you?"

There was a rush of movement, and it occurred to me that I was sticking my nose in where it didn't belong. I chided myself for being so curious. However, I prided myself for being the best detective on the force and gathering information was part of my job. By overhearing this conversation I'd uncovered a valuable piece of information. Someone else didn't like what Monica was doing.

I made a mental note of it for future reference.

As stealthily as possible, I tiptoed back to my room and closed the door, but not before seeing the doorknob of the room across the hall turn.

I mulled the conversation over and over in my mind as I collapsed onto bed. If it was Monica and Lily, maybe I should have intervened. But who was the man? It was an absurd idea and I quickly brushed it aside. Why stick my nose in someone else's problems? No sooner had I began to relax, than the sound of something heavy falling down the stairs brought me upright.

A moment later, someone rushed past my door. I was on my feet in an instant. With my hand on the doorknob, Rose's words halted my movements. I held my breath, waiting, listening.

After a century of seconds, I released the air from my lungs and inhaled. Whatever happened was none of my business. Backing away, I slid between the sheets and let sleep enfold me. As I drifted off to sleep, the deep tones of the grandfather clock registered in the dark recesses of my mind. In my twilight state I couldn't tell if it was twelve gongs or eleven.

It didn't matter.

It was none of my business.

Chapter Eight

Between copious amounts of alcohol and an evening fraught with controversy, Rafael found it difficult to concentrate.

Trudging to his room, he tossed his blazer on the bed and slumped next to it. Blurry visions of Monica's face kept floating to the surface of his mind. Her throaty laughter, her threats, her attempt at blackmailing him haunted him. But it was her wild eyes that bothered him the most.

Had he lost control?

He wasn't sure and that bothered him.

As much as he hated mixing booze with prescriptions, he needed to maintain control.

It was always about control.

Without thinking, he reached into his shirt pocket and pulled out a small container. It was the medication a private doctor had prescribed for his *condition*, as he called it.

He popped two Vraylar pills into his mouth and dry swallowed them. The once-a-day medication was meant to control his frequent episodes of acute manic depression and wild mood swings. It worked most of the time.

Tonight it didn't.

$$$

"Rafael, you need to leave." Hearing Luciano's voice caused him to jolt upright. He'd been so out of it that he failed to hear his old friend enter his room.

Blinking away the cobwebs, he tried to focus. It was eleven-thirty-five, but for the life of him, he couldn't remember the last half hour. He cursed under his breath. With effort, he stood and crossed the room to a mirror and small basin. He peered into its faded reflection. Staring back at him was an old man; his tie hung loose around his neck, his shirt was partially unbuttoned, his blazer lay rumpled on the bed. His hands trembled slightly as he splashed cold water on his face, and dried it with a towel.

"Rafael ... now!" Luciano's tone was urgent.

Grabbing his blazer, he forced his arms through the sleeves and followed his host. He'd taken only a few steps down the stairs when he realized why the sudden urgency. The white sheet covering a human shape told him he needed to hurry and leave before the police arrived.

Sanchez's driver—an experienced chauffeur—knew the best way to get down the mountain without being spotted. He drove the dark limo a short distance from the house and parked in a secluded lot. After a few minutes, two sets of headlights swept by. Once he was sure the coast was clear, he flicked on his headlights, pulled the vehicle onto the road, and headed in the direction of the private airstrip.

Chapter Nine

After ushering Sanchez out through the service entrance, Luciano returned to his room to wait. The Pacific storm which blew from the mountains to the west finally relented leaving the hill country soaked and glistening in the moonlight.

The calm after the storm did little to lighten Luciano's foul mood, however. Standing on his balcony, he inhaled the moist air and let it out slowly. Glancing up, he took in the dazzling sight unfolding overhead. A velvet sky studded with glittering diamonds stood silent witness, and a full moon, now free from its shroud, cast a golden hue over the wide-open grasslands surrounding the mountain residence. If there is a God, He surely knew what He was doing when He painted that mural, Luciano mused.

Two sets of amber headlights cut through goulash pockets of fog drawing his attention. The first vehicle was driven by Sheriff Dusty Mullins. Both he and his deputy were on the take from Luciano's coffers, yet they had a duty to perform no matter where the crime took place. That didn't assuage the jitters he felt as he watched them wind their way along the narrow driveway leading to his home. A second vehicle was driven by the coroner and his assistant.

$$$

As expected, the two official vehicles rolled to a stop.

Four uniformed men climbed out and stretched in the brisk morning air. "Wish I was in bed instead of here," Deputy Coffee complained. His breath created short puffs of condensation. The sheriff grunted his consent and stepped toward the front door. His deputy, the medical examiner, and assistant followed.

Sheriff Mullins rang the doorbell and waited in silence.

Carnes stepped to the door and swung it open. A warm glow illuminated four grim-faced officials. "Good evening, gentlemen. Please, step in," he gave the sheriff a slight bow and backed up.

A moment later, Luciano Beretta appeared. His face showed the strain of the evening. "Good eve … uh … good morning, fellas, Sorry to have to call you out on such a sensitive matter."

Luciano gave Carnes a dismissive nod, but he remained within earshot.

The divot between the sheriff's eyes deepened. Setting aside any formality, he said, "Where's the body?"

As a no-nonsense lawman, Sheriff Mullins was used to seeing death, but not like that of the beautiful woman under the sheet. He knelt to observe the body, then dropped the corner of the covering, stood, and peered around. "What time was the body discovered?" His eyes scanned the faces of the butler who'd found her, the maid who'd covered her, and Luciano, the man who secretly rejoiced in her demise.

Carnes, the stoic butler, stood erect in the face of the sheriff's question. "Sir, I found Miss Monica around eleven-thirty. All the guests had retired for the evening and I was going about my routine, locking doors and turning off lights when I —"

"Can you give me an exact time?" the sheriff interrupted.

Carnes stiffened. "No, sir, not exactly. As I was saying, when I arrived in the grand hall, there she was ... dead as a—"

"That will be all Carnes!" Luciano growled, obviously annoyed by his cavalier reference to death.

The elderly butler nodded to the sheriff and backed away.

Sheriff Mullins turned his gaze to the maid. She shrank under his searching eyes, obviously hoping he wouldn't ask for her green card. She fidgeted with her apron, rolling it between her shaking fingers and releasing it.

"What is your name?"

The maid took a shaky breath. "My name is Rosa Tampico."

The sheriff jotted her name on his notepad, then looked up. "Miss Tampico, did you see anything or hear anything?"

She glanced at her boss.

He nodded.

Swallowing hard, she looked at the sheriff. In broken English, she said, "I see notting; but I heard one ting."

Pencil to pad, the sheriff waited for her to finish. "What did you hear, and when did you hear it?"

Again, she glanced in Luciano's direction. He nudged her forward with a nod.

"It was before I carry a tray of cookies to the game room. I hear two women argue. That's all."

"When did you hear this?"

"I was in the kishen. I not look at clock. I guess maybe ... eleven-tirty, maybe later. I not sure."

Sensing he'd extracted everything he was going to get from the maid, the sheriff turned to Luciano.

"Well, that leaves you, Mr. Beretta. What do you know?"

Beretta, not intimidated by the sheriff, shrugged and looked at the sheet. "I can't tell you anything more about Monica's death than you already know. She'd been drinking, and apparently lost her balance, fell down the stairs, hit her head on the way down and broke her neck."

The medical examiner stepped between the sheriff and Luciano. "Sirs, would you mind taking this matter up in the dining room? I need to get some pictures, make my examination, and check for evidence?"

"Evidence?" Luciano questioned. "It's obvious the poor girl was too drunk to make it up the stairs and fell; that's all. No need to blow this out of proportion."

The lines around the medical examiner's eyes wrinkled. "All the more reason to be thorough. You never know what you might find." He turned and nodded to his assistant.

Sheriff Mullins touched Beretta on the elbow. "Come along, Mr. Beretta. I would like to question your guests.

Have them assemble in the dining room in about ten minutes. Oh, and by the way, whose car was it that left before we arrived?"

Luciano's jaw dropped. "Car? Left?"

"Yes, there was a dry space in the parking lot, meaning someone left after it rained. So who was it?"

Luciano counted the ticks of the clock before giving his answer. He pushed out a weak smile, "Oh that, of course. We were without power, and our cell phones were dead. I sent my son Antonio down the mountain to the nearest store to call you."

Mullins made a note of it, smiled, and glanced up. "And where is Antonio now?"

As if on cue, Carnes stepped forward and cleared his throat, "Mr. Beretta, I'm afraid you're mistaken. As you'll remember, Antonio was in no condition to drive. I sent Benito, your groundskeeper, to make the call."

Luciano nodded and smiled. "Oh yes, that's right. I'd forgotten. Sorry, Sheriff."

The sheriff's eyes narrowed and shifted between the two men. "All right then. Let's have a crack at your guests."

Chapter Ten

Heavy pounding on my door brought me to an upright position.

Muttering, I glared at the clock. Its mocking face read twelve-thirty. I stumbled across the icy hardwood floor, threw the dead-bolt back and peered out. My eyes were met with those of the gate guard. They were red from sleep deprivation. The observation gave me no solace. *Apparently interrupting people's sleep must be his specialty.*

"What's going on?" I demanded, not hiding my irritation.

"We need you downstairs in five minutes," the guard growled.

Turning, he stomped in the direction of the next door without explanation or apology.

It was obvious I was not going to gain any information from him. I slammed the door shut and got dressed. After checking myself out in the mirror, I finger combed my hair and left the room.

$$$

Exactly five minutes later, the other bleary-eyed guests and I assembled around a large mahogany table.

Carnes, wearing a crisply ironed uniform, entered, bearing a silver tray with a carafe of fresh hot coffee and hot water for tea. He set the tray on the credenza, then backed away.

"Is everyone here?" the sheriff asked.

Luciano appraised the group before turning his attention to the sheriff. "Mullins, stop with the theatrics. Of course we're all here."

The sheriff counted noses, made another note on his pad, and proceeded to the first guest. "Madam, would you state your name for the record?"

The elderly woman sitting at the head of the table straightened and looked at the sheriff. She made no attempt to hide her annoyance at being roused from a good night's sleep. Her crotchety voice carried a nonplussed tone. "My name is Rose Beretta, Luciano's mother. And to answer your second question, no, I didn't hear a thing."

"I see," the sheriff said. "And did you observe anything last night that would lead you to believe Miss Peterson was murdered?"

"Murdered?" the word rippled around the table like windswept leaves.

"Yes, murdered," his tone remained level.

Rose's eyes scanned the table and stopped at me. Then she blinked. "No, can't say I did. Now may I return to my bed? You wouldn't want to deprive an old woman of her well-deserved sleep, now would you?"

Out maneuvered by the foxy old woman, the sheriff bowed and let her pass from his presence.

Just before she disappeared, he said, "Miss Rose, is your bedroom on the first floor or the second floor?"

"It is on the first floor. Why do you ask?"

Giving the woman a casual shrug, Mullins smiled. "No reason, I just needed that information for my report."

Turning to Cami, he asked the same questions.

"I didn't see or hear anything. I was in the lounge, drinking coffee." A coy smile played on her lips as she glanced in my direction.

"Was anyone else with you who could verify that?" the sheriff probed.

"Why yes. I was with a couple of friends," pointing to two women draped in silk robes. They confirmed her statement.

"Okay. What was your relationship to Miss Peterson?"

"Relationship? I had no relationship with *Miss Peterson*" she said, her tone etched in ice. "We worked together, that's all. And she was not a Miss. She was married to that man over there." She pointed to Nate. "Why don't you ask him who might have wanted her dead? I'm sure he knows a lot more about Monica than I do."

She stood, walked to the credenza, and poured a cup of coffee. The aroma of fresh brewed coffee wafted across the room. With a grand gesture, she returned to her seat and plopped down.

The sheriff's face reddened as he realized he was about to question the city's public defender. Finally, he drew in a tight breath and said to Nate. "Well?"

"Okay, okay," he said, his fake western twang drifting through the air. "As you know, I'm Nate Peterson, and no, I didn't hear a thang. A few other guys and I were in the game room watching a ball game." He looked around the table for support. A few heads nodded their consent, and the sheriff let out an exasperated sigh.

"Was there anything ... anything that would give anyone reason to believe your wife was murdered?"

Nate's eyes cut to his left before returning to the sheriff's steady gaze. He bit back a half grin. "Murdered. I'd dare say everyone in this room who knew Monica probably had a reason to kill her. She was a conniving, back-stabbing ..."

"That will be all, Mr. Peterson," Luciano said with a wave of his hand. "You see, Sheriff, Monica wasn't a very nice woman. But in order for someone to kill her, they had to have opportunity; and we all have an alibi. I, and the gov ... uh, a few of the guys were in the men's den relaxing over a drink and a cigar. Nate and a few others were in the game room. Cami and the rest of the women were in the lounge. We are all accounted for unless you count Mr. O'Reilly, better known as Inspector O'Reilly."

I jumped to my feet, "Inspector! When did that happen?"

Luciano leaned back in his chair. A smile stretched across his face. "Oh, I heard rumors. Now, if you need help with an alibi ..."

He let his statement dangle like a carrot on a string as if to say, 'if he needs an alibi, I've got one, and then he's mine. If he doesn't take my offer, the sheriff can have him. Either way, he's cooked'

Squaring my shoulders, I addressed the sheriff directly. "No Sheriff, I have no alibi. I was alone in my room."

His eyes appraised me for a moment. "And where did you get those nasty scratches?"

Stupid me, I had failed to roll down my sleeves after getting dressed. The arteries in my neck throbbed. Clearing my throat, I glanced down and sighed. "I know what it looks like but I can assure you, I got these chasing a lost golf ball."

A rustle of muffled snickers scattered across the room like mischievous children.

The sheriff's eyes narrowed as he looked around. "Do any of you remember seeing those scratches earlier this evening?" His question hung like the blade of a guillotine about to drop. No one spoke.

He returned his gazed to me. "Trace, you know the routine, but I gotta ask ya. What was your relationship with the deceased?"

I paused as a thousand bitter memories coalesced into a grotesque shape in my mind. "Look, I'm the detective around here. I know where this is going."

"Just answer the question, Mr. Hot-shot Detective."

I held his gaze for another beat. "We were married for two years. It ended in an ugly divorce."

"Have you seen much of your ex-wife since then?"

"No, sir. This was the first time since the divorce."

"And what happened when you two met?"

My heart pounded like a hammer against my ribs. My palms slicked, and I rubbed them on my pants. "To be frank, it was uncomfortable." I let my voice trail off.

"Did you two argue?"

"Call it a moment of intense fellowship."

A ripple of suppressed laughter percolated behind me.

"I saw Mr. O'Reilly sneaking down the hall real guilty like about the time of the murder," Maurice Rivera blurted.

Heads turned to face the source of the outburst.

Maurice grinned broadly.

"Well, Mr. O'Reilly? Got anything to say before I read you your rights?" the sheriff asked. A smug grin stretched across his stubbly face.

I knew I'd been in the hall and listened in on two people's conversation. But kill Monica? Never. But to admit my proximity to the crime was paramount to a confession. It would confirm the sheriff's growing suspicion. If I denied it, it would only look worse. My hesitation was all Sheriff Mullins needed.

Shifting from one foot to the other, Mullins nodded to his deputy, then back to me. "Sir, I need you to come with me down to headquarters for additional questions. The rest of you, please give my deputy your contact information and don't leave town. I might ask you a few more questions."

He walked over and placed a set of steel bracelets on my wrists all the while reciting my Miranda rights.

"You sure you don't need an alibi, Trace?" Luciano asked, interrupting the sheriff and cutting his eyes toward one of the women.

I felt my face blanch. It would be suicide to accept Luciano's offer, and we both knew it. I pinched my eyes shut and shook my head.

As we neared the door, Mrs. Beretta returned from her room and hobbled over to the sheriff. "Sheriff, did I mention that I had a pleasant conversation with this nice young man?"

The sheriff stopped and peered over his shoulder, waiting for the cagey woman to make her point. "Why no, Mrs. Beretta, you didn't."

"Well, I did," she croaked.

"And?"

"And it means nothing, except to say I saw those scratches on his arms hours before the alleged murder. So turn him loose."

The sheriff, knowing he was outsmarted again, let out a slow breath.

"You don't say. Are you sure you saw those marks? Cause it certainly would make my job a whole lot easier."

The elderly woman moved within inches of the sheriff's chest and jabbed her gnarled finger against his badge. "I don't give diddley squat about making your job easier. I saw what I saw, so let him go."

Sheriff Mullins leaned back and placed his hands on his hips. "I appreciate what you're doing Mrs. Beretta, but Mr. O'Reilly practically admitted he killed his ex-wife. He has motive and opportunity, and I have circumstantial evidence." He held up a plastic bag with a button from my coat the medical examiner had discovered in Monica's hand. "Now step aside and let me do my job. We'll let the courts decide if he's innocent or guilty."

The moisture in my mouth turned to dust as I eyed the incriminating evidence. How did that button get in my deceased, ex-wife's hand? My mind raced. I'd been setup and now I'm going to pay.

As they pushed me into the police cruiser, I turned and nodded to Rose. She offered me an apologetic smile, and then the door slammed shut.

Luciano stepped over to his mother, slid his arm around her slender waist, and pulled her close. As he tugged her back from the car, I heard him say, "Well, you tried, Mother. That's all you could do."

Moments later, the police cruiser pulled away and disappeared in the morning fog.

Chapter Eleven

5 years later ...

Thinking back, my arrest and subsequent trial were all a blur.

Nate Peterson did his best to bring the full weight of the judicial system down upon me. In the trial of State vs. Trace O'Reilly, he used his surrogates in the District Attorney's department to level every false charge they could muster. On the witness stand, Nate flaunted the fact that it was his wife's murder I was accused of committing.

Circumstantial evidence was bandied about as fact, like red meat before a ravenous wolf. The argument, overheard by Nate himself, the confrontation in the hall, also overheard by Nate and others, the fact that I had no alibi, Maurice Rivera's testimony that he'd observed me in the hall during the time of the alleged murder, and the damning button from my coat found in Monica's cold, dead hand, sealed my doom. In his closing argument, the prosecuting attorney, one of Nate's golfing buddies, called for the maximum penalty under the law ... death by lethal injection. But he made it clear, in his opinion; it was too merciful for the likes of me.

It took the jury less than five hours to return a verdict. Guilty on all charges.

Nate tried unsuccessfully to mask his pleasure as the jury was polled. It was unanimous. After the verdict was read, his impassioned plea for the death penalty was one of vitriol. If it were anyone but me, I would have stood up and applauded his eloquence, his passion, his fire-in-the-belly oratory. But alas, it was me who stood next to my less-than-competent public defender feeling the weight of false guilt when the judge finally read my fate.

Mercifully, the trial ended and I was led away to Pelican Bay State Prison. PBSP, often referred to as Supermax, is California's maximum-security prison, a sprawling 275-acre facility located in Del Norte County, California.

For the next four years, I watched inmates come and go with regularity. Some died of old age and disease, others from fights, and a few on good behavior. The others, like me, lived in limbo. Our attorneys, usually state-appointed public defenders, labored relentlessly on our behalf often going to great lengths to prove we had been sufficiently rehabilitated and ready to be released into society. In most cases, the parole board saw through the ruse. Even so, that didn't stop them from trying until they used up all their appeals. Now they, like me, sat on death row waiting execution.

Execution ... just the thought of it gave me nightmares. The idea of being strapped down on a gurney, like a sheep before her shearers, and being wheeled into an observatory where spectators waited on the other side of a large window, brought on cold sweats. And then to watch a technician jab needles into my arm and wait for three noxious poisons to surge through the tubes until they reached my heart and lungs, effectively stopping them, wasn't appealing.

Not at all.

But that was my future.

The recent California high court decision, to keep a key provision in Proposition 66 calling for speedy executions, failed to impose strict deadlines. A subsequent Supreme Court decision reversed an eleven-year hiatus, thus opening the way to resume executions. My relocation to San Quinton State Prison, which housed the state's only death chamber, told me my last appeal had failed.

Unconsciously, I began to count the days. The Bible tells us to number our days. I took that literally, however. The one thing worse than death, was waiting for it … and I was tired of the wait. To me, it would be a relief to get it over. I had long since given up any hope of a reprieve from the governor. That was never going to happen. My only hope now was in the saving grace of my Savior. The decision to trust Christ a few years before my incarceration was what sustained me through the long nights and even longer days in maximum security. And it gave me reason to go on, even into the death chamber.

Chapter Twelve

The view from the narrow cell window on death row hadn't changed much in the last year and probably wouldn't.

If it did, I wouldn't see it.

Except for the four seasons, rain or shine, the grand mountain nestled among its kin was a constant source of stability—something I'd not had in my formative years. I'd always hoped to climb that mountain, smell the crisp, clean air, feel the icy rocks beneath my feet, and enjoy the spectacular view from its lofty height. But that would never be. My confinement in the maximum-security facility was about to end, and not as I'd hoped … or prayed. I'd come to grips with the sad fact that my life was about to end, and I was determined to face it like a man.

The electronic snap of a door lock brought me from my reverie. Warden Harper's voice beckoned my attention. I turned. Filling the doorway to my five by seven cell was the warden flanked by two burly guards. The grim-faced man whom I'd come to respect stood, giving me time to step forward on my own volition.

Funny thing, here I am on death-row, where every move is regulated from the time I rise in the morning to the time I go to bed, and now they're giving me time to decide whether to leave my cell on my own or go under duress.

With a nonchalant shrug, I stepped forward, held out my hands, and waited. The guards, moving with precision, shackled my wrists to a waist-chain and did the same to my feet. I wondered if they'd ever thought about where I'd go if I chose to run. It was lunacy for me to entertain such an idea for even a moment.

I had already been served my last meal: steak and potatoes. The steak was tough and the potatoes over-cooked. But what the heck, I figured … *it was free.* I ate it in solitude with a plastic knife and fork which the kitchen staff provided.

The only other break from my routine was a visit from the Chaplain. His nonsensical drivel about praying for my departing soul meant nothing, but I appreciated that one last human conversation. My decision to place my faith in Jesus while in rehab, years earlier, was good enough, yet it felt good to sit and listen to the Chaplain read the Twenty-Third Psalm. The Chaplain's parting comment, however, left me wondering if he was really a man of the cloth.

"Have you read the *Procedure Manual?*" the warden asked softly, bringing me back to the stark reality of the moment.

I nodded sullenly, not wanting to answer and attempting to suppress my angst.

"Any questions? I mean, you do understand what's about to take place, don't you?"

I sighed. "Yes and no."

Harper cocked his head. "What do you mean?"

His question brought a smile to my face, the first in days. With a partial grin, I said, "Yes, I read your stupid manual, and no, I don't have any questions."

The warden turned and followed the guards as they led me down the long corridor. My chains jangled in an inane rhythm on the tile floor announcing yet another cell-mate was walking the Green Mile—one which they all expected to walk.

As I duck-walked past the other inmates, the chain caught on my flip-flop causing me to stumble.

"Careful," the guard said as he caught me by the arm. "We don't want you to get all banged up. Now, do we?" His firm grip kept me from falling and making a fool of myself. His warm hand gave me support and strength.

In the background, I heard the snickers and jeers of men I'd come to know only by their nicknames. Rocky, in particular, was one I avoided at all costs. His penetrating black orbs seethed with hatred. As I clanged passed his cell, he flung a string of curses at me.

"Ignore him," the warden cautioned. "He's just jealous you're getting out before him."

Getting out of here?

I guess he was right in a way.

Focusing on the door at the end of the hall, I kept walking.

Finally, we reached a metal door and stopped. Not speaking, we waited for the electronic lock to give us permission to enter.

"Say, Warden ..."

He turned around to face me. His eyes were ringed with tears and I felt his compassionate gaze. "Yes, Trace?"

"What did ya think of the Chap's last statement?"

"I don't know. I wasn't there. What did he say?"

"He said if I refused the church's way, I'd have to go to purgatory until I learned my lesson."

The warden's eyebrows knit. "Well, Son, I've heard other condemn ... uh, other men tell me that."

"Do you believe in purgatory? I was taught that there is only heaven and hell." My matter-of-fact statement caused the two guards to exchange glances.

A moment later, an electronic snap announced the opening of the last door between me and eternity.

The warden leaned closer and whispered, "If I were you, I'd be prepared for anything ... anything."

His last words sent an icy chill down my spine.

Taking a cautious step, we entered the brightly lit chamber, and the steel door behind us closed with a resounding thud. Next to a gurney stood a stainless steel table bearing a tray. I blinked away the vision before it registered...

A gurney occupied the center of the room. I noticed the crisp, clean sheets on it—a welcome contrast to the rumpled ones I'd left back in my cell.

Next to the gurney stood two stoic orderlies prepared to take ownership of the last minutes of my life. Together, they helped me get into position.

"Comfortable?" one asked.

I nodded, not speaking.

The question seemed odd since within a short time, it wouldn't matter. As they made the final preparations, I stared up at the fluorescent lights wondering what it was going to be like at the end. I suddenly felt nauseous and was glad there wasn't much in my stomach to give up.

With rigid determination, I endured the humiliation of being 'prepped' for the 'procedure,' as the warden called it. "Procedure ... " I cursed, under my breath. As merciful as it was, it still was taking an innocent man's life.

Once the orderlies had completed their task, they rolled me into the 'Room.' To my left hung a bank of tubes ... I knew what they were for. To my right was a drawn curtain. It was obvious what that covered. In some morbid way, I was the star of the show. I just hoped the observation room was empty. This was a private matter, and I didn't want anyone cheering my departure. Either way, it didn't matter anymore.

My audience awaited me.

Knowing my death would provide the grieving family with a little satisfaction, I prayed for grace to face them with courage. I'd hoped it might bring them closure.

But I knew the truth.

Somewhere out there was a murderer. My only involvement in the crime was to provide the police with an easy "catch." I was in the wrong place, at the wrong time, with no alibi. By a stroke of bad luck, I happened to have a set of fresh scratches on my forearms and that cursed button sealed my fate.

I often wondered about the two female voices I'd heard down the hall. When I mentioned it to my attorney, he brushed it aside saying, "It could have been anybody. There were people everywhere."

I didn't blame him, however. My last attorney was competent, just not very convincing. My drinking problem and subsequent bitter divorce were enough to turn my staunchest supporters against me.

The Valium they'd given me earlier did little to staunch the adrenalin rush I was feeling. Taking a ragged breath, I closed my eyes and tried to relax. I tried to focus on that mountain, now further from my reach than ever. I remembered reading a verse in the Bible about the mountain of the Lord. *Maybe there will be mountains in heaven. I sure hope so.*

With my eyes closed, I followed the movements of the technicians until it got quiet. I wasn't sure if it was the meds or my imagination, but I felt myself drifting … floating.

Gradually, everything around me became peaceful.

Then everything went black.

Chapter Thirteen

The mountain air was exactly as I had expected it to be—fresh and clean and a far cry from the stale air of my cell on death row.

The higher I climbed, the more my legs burned. Yet, I pressed on. *Too much sitting around in the cell. Oh well, the hike will do me good.* With increased effort, I pushed myself to new heights. An icy wind bit into my exposed flesh and shards of rock cut my bare hands. Why am I barefoot? I wondered.

"Trace! Trace! Wake up!"

I heard my name echoing across barren cliffs. Lifting my eyes, I squinted in the direction of the sound. On a rocky outcropping stood a man, his arms waving wildly. Finding a path, I quickened my steps and hiked closer. When I finally reached the precipice, the blinding sunlight burned my eyes, and I lifted my hand to block the glare. I blinked a few times, trying to grasp the vision.

Someone was shaking my shoulder attempting to wake me. As my mind cleared, I saw Warden Harper towering over me. I was still strapped to the gurney, but I was alive. The syringes had been removed from my arm, and a doctor held an oxygen mask over my face.

"Trace, can you hear me?" His words echoed just out of reach.

"Am I dead?"

"No, Trace." Harper leaned closer.

"Can you sit up?"

"Uh, yeah, I think. You're not the devil, and you're certainly not God, so where am I?" I muttered through the mask.

"Get that dang thing off him, Doc. This is an emergency," the warden barked.

The doctor quickly complied as the warden unstrapped me. With the warden's help, I sat up, still dazed.

"Looks like you've got a new lease on life, son," the Warden said, offering me a bright smile.

I shook my head, trying to clear the cob-webs. "Meaning what?"

"Your alibi, Mrs. Beretta, she finally came through for you. On her deathbed, she insisted that the governor hear her testimony. She convinced him you were innocent, and he signed your release just minutes ago. You were already unconscious when your sentence was commuted, but they were able to stop the process."

The warden picked up a set of street clothes, handed them to me. Glancing over his shoulder, he said, "Here, try these on."

I wiped the icy sweat from my brow. "Thanks, but I think I'd rather be in heaven now instead of living in this stinking place."

The warden nodded. "Well, that wasn't my call. Apparently, God still has something for you to do."

He pulled back the curtain. "We have a situation," he said as he peered at a mob on the other side of the observation window. One of the inmates held Lily by the throat. A filthy grin stretched across his face. Another inmate held Nate at gunpoint.

"While you were in here, some of the inmates got loose and rioted."

"They're screaming for your immediate release," the doctor added, handing me a bottle of water. "Here, drink this. It will help clear your head."

I took the bottle, twisted off the lid, and lifted it to my lips. After taking a few swigs, I swished the water around in my mouth, then spat it out. The drugs left a foul taste in my mouth. Wiping my lips with the sleeve of my shirt, I glanced at the mob. "I didn't know I was so popular."

The warden yanked the curtains shut, "You're not, but Rocky wants you for himself.

"Reggie Ramirez? What's he want with me?" I asked, slipping on a pair of Crocs.

"Do you remember old Mike?"

"Yeah. What about him?"

"You remember saving him from a hazing when he first came here?" The lines in the warden's face grew deeper.

I let my mind wander back a few months. "Yes, I remember. What about it?"

The warden stole a glance over his shoulder. "Well, Rocky hasn't forgotten it either. Had you been in the general pop, you would have been dead a long time ago. Being on death row probably saved your life."

"Gee thanks, I think." I replied sarcastically. "So what do we do now?"

The warden strode to the exit, "If you want to live, you'd better follow me."

I wobbled to my feet. "But what about Nate and Lily? You can't just leave them."

The warden paused a moment at the threshold of the Death Chamber. "We have a no negotiation policy with the inmates when they riot. They're as good as dead either way. Now follow me."

The warden turned and dashed through the Prep Room and headed toward the exit. I accepted the warden's offer and moved as quickly as my legs allowed. After a few steps, the floor tilted and I grabbed the wall to keep from falling. Taking a few deep breaths, I pushed myself up and closed the distance between me and the warden. When we got to the end of the hall, we found four armed guards waiting, their guns held at the ready. As we ran for the service elevator, a voice broke over the intercom.

"Warden, I have no quarrel with you. But you have someone I'd like to get my hands on. As you can see, I have a couple of people you might be interested in exchanging. So let's play. I'll give you two for one ... your choice."

Harper stopped running. Breathing hard, he put his hands on his knees and leaned against the wall.

"We're waiting," Rocky taunted.

The warden walked to a phone on the wall and lifted the receiver. "Look, Rocky, this is ludicrous. You'll never get away with it. If you release your hostages now, I'll consider letting you off with only a mild warning."

"Nope, not gonna happen. You see, the men look to me as a kinda godfather. If I lose face, they won't respect me. You feel me, man?"

Harper swallowed hard. "I hear you, but—"

Before he could stop me, I grabbed the phone from the warden's shaking hand. "Look Rocky, you let both hostages go, and you can have me. I'll meet you in the cafeteria." Then I slammed the receiver in place before the warden could intervene.

"You know you just signed your death warrant, don't you?" the warden said.

"Like you said, 'God still has something for me to do.' Maybe it's saving Nate and Lily. I've already made my peace with God, so either way: I'm a dead man walking. The Bible says, *'For me to live is Christ and to die is gain.'* So you see Warden, no matter what happens, I win."

Warden Harper shook his head. "That may be so, but I wouldn't recommend going the way Rocky has planned. You're in for a whole lot of hurt if he gets his hands on you."

I took a shaky step toward the door leading to the main facility. "We'll see about that. After what I just went through, I believe with God's help, I can do anything." Giving him one last nod, I opened the door and stepped through it.

The moment the door closed behind me, two powerful hands grabbed me and threw me to the floor. A sweaty T-shirt was jammed over my head, temporarily blinding me. The stench assaulted my nostrils, making my stomach churn. With my head spinning, I forced the bile down my throat. Strong hands grabbed me by the arms and dragged me through the hall.

Chapter Fourteen

V oices rose into jeers as my captor tossed me to the cafeteria floor.

I skidded to a stop and tried to peer through the hood but all I could see was muted images. One of the inmates yanked it from my head and I found myself encircled by angry men. I glanced up. Rocky's hulking figure loomed over me. His arms crossed, his chest heaving. Nate and Lily cowered in a corner. A gun-wielding inmate held them hostage.

"I'm glad you acquiesced to my request," the rogue criminal said. A menacing smile played on his lips.

Before I could get to my feet, Rocky kicked me in the ribs. Streaks of orange and red flashed across my vision. I buckled with the force of the blow and rolled to the other side in a tight circle. Rocky lunged for me, but I, being smaller and more nimble, shifted from his grip. His fist struck the wall, and he let out a string of expletives. With effort, I gained my footing and grabbed a metal chair. As Rocky charged me like a wild bull, I lifted it and brought it down on his head, temporarily stunning him. Rocky toppled over giving me a chance to escape, but the man grabbed me by the ankle and pulled me down.

For several minutes we wrestled, each trying to get the advantage over the other. The big man grabbed my shirt and yanked me forward. Someone stuck out their foot causing me to stumble. I fell and smashed my head into the tile. Seeing stars, I knew what was coming next. Instinctively, I rolled to my left as his powerful fist swished past me. It struck the concrete floor, and he cursed. I felt the man's hot breath and smelled his sweat as we continued to battle to get the upper hand. Remembering a move I'd learned wrestling in high school, I pivoted and got Rocky in a stranglehold. With what little strength I had left, I squeezed until Rocky fell limp. Not knowing if I killed him or not, I released my hold and he tumbled forward. His head smacked the floor with a solid thud and a crimson pool formed from his nose.

Half dazed and spitting blood, I stood and scanned the room. All at once, the door burst open and four armed guards led by Warden Harper stormed the cafeteria, their weapons firing like jackhammers. Fearing I'd get struck, I ducked as bullets ripped through the air. Out of the corner of my eye, I saw Nate squeeze back into the crowd, keeping Lily behind him.

The inmate with the gun froze, caught between shooting his hostages or the guards. A moment later, he buckled as a bullet struck him in the gut. He groaned and toppled over. Another inmate took a bullet to the head and fell, pinning me under him. A circle of steaming blood formed where the man lay.

From my hidden position, I watched Nate grab Lily's hand and tug her behind an overturned table, while the inmates scattered in all directions.

"We have bigger problems now," the warden said as he took control of the cafeteria.

I struggled out from under the newly formed corpse and stood. "Why's that?" I asked. "You freed the hostages, and I'm still alive."

"Yes, but the inmates have overrun the guards in the main hub, and they released all the others. If they get to the armory, none of us will get out of here alive."

Hand against the wall, I grimaced. "I think Rocky broke my ribs."

Nate pushed himself to his feet and pulled Lily up. Glaring at the warden, he said, "Isn't there another way out of here?"

Warden Harper rubbed his chin. "There is, but it's risky and there are no guarantees."

With a quick nod, two guards stepped into the hall and took up flanking positions with the two bringing up the rear. Like a quarterback, Warden Harper plowed ahead with me, Lily, Nate, and the other two guards following close. We reached the service elevator and piled in. Not waiting, the warden hit the down button.

The elevator glided to a stop on the lower level, and the doors relaxed out of sight. Cautiously, one of the guards peered around the corner and gave the all-clear sign. Resuming their previous positions, we ran down the hallway.

A moment later, the air grew thick with lead as Rocky and a cluster of inmates took aim at us.

"They must have gotten to the armory faster than I thought," Harper said, ducking behind a desk.

The remaining guards returned fire, wounding one inmate and killing another. One of the guards spun as a bullet struck his shoulder. Lily screamed and buried her face in Nate's chest. He grabbed her and dashed for a door marked Utility Room.

I glanced at the warden. He nodded, and the two of us sprang in behind Nate and Lily dragging the wounded guard with us. Once in, claustrophobia nagged at my frayed nerves. Although I'd been incarcerated for the last five years in a small cell, I never had to share it with four other people.

Moments before he closed the door, one of the guards tossed his service weapon to Warden Harper. "Here, you may need this."

Harper caught it and slammed the door shut. The stagnant air grew tense as he threw the deadbolt. After checking the magazine, he took a quick peek through the small window in the door.

"What about the guards?" Nate asked.

The warden grimaced. "They are sworn to protect me at all costs. They will stay and fight."

"But what about us? We can't stay here." Nate's voice grew in intensity.

"Don't worry, help will be here soon."

Lily glared at me with angry eyes. "It's all your fault. Now we're all going to die."

"It's not his fault, Lily," the warden said. "You know as well as I do, the governor granted his pardon based on new evidence moments before he was to be executed."

She clenched her fists and stomped. "What difference does it make now anyway? We're still going to die." Dread colored her voice.

For the first time since the ordeal began, Nate acknowledged my presence. "She's right. None of us are getting out of here alive, and we've got you to blame."

"Me!" I protested. "I didn't cause the riot. It was me, if you'll remember, who took on Rocky and beat him."

"Yeah, well. He didn't stay beaten for long. You should have killed him." I recognized the innuendo.

Shots echoed just outside the door as the guards fought for their lives. A heavy thud pounded against the door nearly knocking the warden back.

"I'm not a killer." I fired back through gritted teeth.

The warden peered through the mesh-reinforced glass. His expression told me all I needed to know. The guards were dead, and the inmates were at the door.

One of them rammed his shoulder against it sending vibrations throughout the small space. The air became wire tight as the inmates threatened to break through.

"Young lady, could you step aside?" the warden asked. "You're standing on our only way out of this facility."

She glanced at the manhole cover beneath her feet. Nate shoved her aside and began tugging on its ledge. The warden and I joined him and within a minute, we had the iron cover removed.

Looking down, all I saw was a set of iron foot-holds leading into pitch darkness. "I'll go first," I said, taking a step toward the hole.

"Hold on a danged minute," Nate said, his western drawl returning. "If you think you're gonna leave us here to face those guys, you're crazy. I'm going first."

Without waiting, he disappeared into the darkness followed by Lily. I looked at the warden and shrugged. "That's gratitude for ya."

At the bottom of the shaft, Harper and I reunited with Nate and Lily. They stood in another dimly lit passageway looking confused and frightened. Moss covered the concrete walls and dripped with condensation making the tunnel even scarier than it was.

"This place smells like an outhouse," Lily said, holding her nose.

"That's because this service tunnel connects with the main sewer system," Warden Harper said.

"What good's that going to do us?" Nate asked, peering into the receding light.

The warden let out a frustrated breath. Pointing with his nose, he said, "If we can get to the next level before the inmates, we can exit the facility through the sewer. Now let's get a move on."

As we moved silently through the narrow hall, voices echoed from behind. Harper lifted his hand. We stopped and held our breath.

"What is it?" Nate whispered.

I squinted into the darkness. "It's the inmates. They must have broken through the door and are following us."

Lily moved closer to her step-father and glared at me. "I hate you! First you kill my mother, and now you're going to get us killed."

"Shh! Hold your voice down or they'll hear you," the warden warned.

"Too late, I hear footsteps," I said as we tried to put some distance between us and the crazed inmates.

A deafening blast and a flash of blazing light exploded as Rocky and his men opened fire. Lily shrieked and ducked. Light bulbs shattered overhead sending shards of glass down around us. A moment later, we were engulfed in cold, wet darkness.

"I'm outta here," Lily screamed and dashed down the black tunnel.

"Wait," Nate cried and ran after her.

Warden Harper, an experienced military veteran, took aim at the muzzle flashes and squeezed off a round. Someone groaned, followed by a dull thud.

"At any time S.W.A.T. teams and FBI agents will storm this place," Warden Harper said. "If we get caught down here, it's shoot first, ask questions later. I'll stay and hold the inmates off. You go after those two." He extended his hand to me. "Good luck."

I clasped his hand and squeezed it. "Thanks, sir. You've been a kind and supportive friend, and I'll never forget you."

Another wall of lead zinged overhead and I ducked to keep from getting hit. "Guess you're right about one thing, though."

Harper fired at the flashes. "What do ya mean?"

I leaned close. "The last thing you said before I passed out was, 'If I were you, I'd be prepared for anything.'"

The warden let out a chuckle. "Were you?"

"Yep. How 'bout you?"

Harper's voice grew raspy and low. "I settled that long ago, brother. I'm ready to meet my Maker, and it may be sooner than you."

Chapter Fifteen

"Where are we?" Lily's voice sliced through the darkness.

Nate caught up to her and stopped. He leaned against the wall, his breath coming in short gulps, his mind whirling. "I don't know. The warden was supposed to guide us, but I think we made a wrong turn."

Fingers splayed, Lily felt her way along the slimy walls searching for a door, an escape, anything. Her hand touched a handle, and she pulled. The rusty iron door swung open, its hinges resisting with a piercing squeak.

"Be careful, you never know what's ahead," Nate said as he pushed past her.

Above them, an emergency light cast an amber glow on the small room. They saw a set of circular stairs descend into a black hole.

"I hear water," Lily said, looking down.

"The warden said there was a sewer down here. I guess he knew what he was talking about. Let's go."

He began the slow descent with Lily close behind him. The stairs groaned and vibrated with each step but held. Its cold, wet iron railing sent chills up Nate's arms as he picked his way further from the failing light. When he reached the bottom, he stepped off into waist-deep water. The current swirling around nearly knocked him off his feet, and he clung tightly to the ladder.

"This isn't good. There must have been a flash flood in the hills to send this much water down here."

Lily hovered on the last step. "I'm scared. I want to go back."

"We can't go back, Lily. Who knows what those men might do if they get their filthy hands on you. We need to keep going." He held her hand as she stepped off the ladder into the water.

A moment later, Nates' feet slipped and the two of them were swept along with the current like logs in a flume. Lily's cries for help were drowned out by the noisy rush of water.

$$$

In the darkness, I heard movement followed by heavy breathing.

Bracing myself, I prepared to clobber whoever approached.

"Mr. Warden sur, it's me, Big Mike. Don't shoot." His breath came in short gulps. "I've been hunting for you all over the place."

"Well, you found me, now what?" Harper said.

"I'm here to hep Mr. Trace escape."

Harper couldn't keep from laughing at the large black man's candor. "Big Mike, he doesn't need to escape. He's been pardoned. Didn't you hear?"

"Yep, I heard, but by the looks of it, he ain't goin' nowhere 'sept, I hep him."

I couldn't help but chuckle at the absurdity of the situation. Here I was, a free man depending on an inmate to get me out of prison. "I think he's got a point, Warden. What about it?"

Warden Harper didn't miss a beat. "Look Mike. If you promise to help us and not make a run for it, I'll personally vouch for your early release."

"Ah sur, you don't needs to do that. I kinda likes it here. Plus I have me a little Bible study group, and I'd hate to miss it."

All at once, a large figure emerged from the shadows. It was Rocky and he lunged for me cursing and swinging an iron pipe. Big Mike caught it and yanked it from the man's hand. Rocky threw himself at me but Big Mike caught him by the neck.

"Hey, dude." Big Mike's baritone voice echoed off the slippery walls. "Don't go beatin' up my friend."

He raised the iron pipe and brought it down on Rocky's head. His eyes bulged, then rolled back in his head and he toppled over with a sickening thud. "I don't' s'pose you'll be lettin' him out on good behavior, now will ya, Warden?" Big Mike chuckled.

Warden Harper grinned and shook his head. "No, I don't s'pose so."

Another round of bullets ricocheted off the walls causing all of us to flatten behind Rocky's bulky frame.

"I've got about six rounds left," the warden whispered. "I'll hold them off as long as I can. Now go."

I patted him on the shoulder and pushed off into the darkness with Big Mike close behind.

Seeing a dim, amber glow coming from an entrance, I scurried forward. "This way," I said and began to descend the same rusty stairs Lily and Nate had taken minutes earlier.

As Big Mike pressed his weight on the steps, it groaned, threatening to break loose. "What's that?" he yelled.

"I think it's the ladder. We're not going to make it."

As I spoke, the bolts holding it to the wall released their grip. A gut-wrenching scream sliced through the air as the ladder buckled sending us plunging into the icy water below. It struck the bottom of the sewer with a jolt knocking me clear but pinned Mike's legs. Muddy water washed over his head, threatening to drown him as I fought to cling to a single handhold.

"Mike, hold on. Let me see if I can get your legs free."

He groaned in pain and spit out a mouth full of water. "No sur, I've had it. My legs are caught in the twisted metal. Even if you could get them out, I can't swim."

A dark wave splashed me in the face. I came up sputtering. "No! I won't leave you."

"Mr. Trace. What you did fa me when I came here was the first act of kindness any white man had ever showed me. I swore right then I wanted to be like you. You showed me the way to God, and I'm ready to meet Him. Now go save Miss Lily."

Another surge of water swept over Mike's head, pushing him down.

"Mike! Mike!" my cries went unanswered.

For uncounted minutes, I grappled with the ladder trying to free my friend's legs. Finally, after I knew it was too late, I gave up.

"Oh God, why?" I yelled over the pounding surge. "Six good men have died to save me, and I'm not letting anyone else die on my account."

I had to save Lily. Even if it meant saving Nate, the man who sent me to this Hell-hole, then so be it.

As my hands weakened in the icy waters, a large chunk of wood appeared out of nowhere. It rushed me like a locomotive, nearly knocking me off my feet. In desperation, I reached out and grabbed it. Immediately, I was swept away in the current.

Further ahead, I heard faint cries for help. I hoped it was Big Mike but the closer I got to the voices, the more it sounded like two people.

In a flash, I rushed past Nate and Lily who desperately clung to an outcropping of wires. Releasing the log, I grabbed the mesh and held on.

"Trace. Lily's legs are caught on something. Can you help her?" Nate shouted as a wave splashed in his face. He came up sputtering. "I don't know how much longer I can hold on."

Lily's head bobbed beneath the water, and she came up spitting.

As I fought my way closer, I felt the heat of Lily's eyes glowing at me. She hates me. I can feel it, I said to myself, but it doesn't matter. She's my daughter, and I'm going to save her.

Without hesitation, I ducked beneath the torrent and felt for her legs. A large cable had wrapped itself around her right ankle like a python. My lungs screamed for oxygen, and I had to come up for a breath. "I think I can get it. Hold still."

Grabbing another gulp of air, I dove back down. The frigid water numbed my fingers and dug into my exposed flesh. Ignoring the discomfort, I felt for the end of the cable. Once I found it, I began to loosen it so Lily could break free. Every fiber of my being screamed for air, but I refused to yield to the temptation to exhale. If I did, my next breath would spell certain death. Moments before I blacked out, the cable relaxed its grip and I yanked Lily's leg free.

With a push, I kicked my feet and broke the surface, gasping for air.

"Nate, Lily."

They were gone ... swept further down the sewer. I took a few seconds to catch my breath before yielding to the current. Lying on my back, I allowed myself to be pushed along following the log. The waters had risen nearly to the top of the uneven ceiling, and I had to be careful not to hit my head on the caged light bulbs. I knew if I didn't get out of the sewer soon, I never would.

Looking ahead, I saw a light. It was the sewer drain. I breathed a sigh of relief, hoping it dumped into the holding tank.

With a bone-jarring thud, I smashed into Nate and Lily and realized they were pinned against an iron grate. The log I had ridden earlier bumped mindlessly on the barrier like a battering ram.

"Nate, grab the other end of that log and let's use it to pry the gate open."

He nodded without argument and together we fought against the current. After struggling for several minutes, we were able to pry the rusty bars apart enough for each one of us to squeeze through.

"Lily, you go first. I'll hold it back," I said between gulps of water and air.

Not looking back, she pushed through the narrow gap and was carried downstream into what appeared to be a large retaining pool.

"Nate, you go next. Then hold it so I can get out, okay?"

Nate needed no encouragement. He quickly shimmied between the iron bars and the concrete opening and began to swim to the far bank.

"Thanks a lot," I muttered.

Out of the darkness, Big Mike's corpse appeared and slammed into the grate. The hinges bowed, then yielded. A moment later, Mike's body and I surged through the opening followed by the log. Thankful for Big Mike's help, I swam to the other side.

Nate and Lily stood shivering in the cold.

"If it weren't for you, none of this would have happened!" Lily snarled. Her words stinging like acid.

Wiping the mud from my eyes, I looked at them with pity. "It's all right. One day, I'll prove I didn't kill your mother."

"And how are you going to do that?" She spat.

My mind whirled. It had been nearly six years since my trial. All the evidence had been sifted through with unrivaled scrutiny, yet I'd been found guilty. It was only Rose Beretta's testimony that saved my life. And if the report was true, she was dead. I needed hard evidence to convince Lily … to convince the world.

I needed to find my ex-wife's killer.

Chapter Sixteen

A fter our daring escape, I found myself alone, broke and homeless.

Returning to civilian life was a lot harder than I'd imagined. I tried picking up the shattered pieces of my life but found it wasn't worth the effort. It was time to start a new life. Forgetting the past, however, didn't include forgetting Lily.

One late fall day I took the bus to Sacramento Junior College where Lily attended classes. When I arrived, I found the campus bustling with activity. While some students sat on concrete benches, others lounged under the shade of large oak trees. Still, others moved along the sidewalks with purpose. With their back-packs bouncing lightly on their shoulders, they walked or rode their bicycles to some unknown destination.

As I strolled from building to building trying to look inconspicuous, I suddenly felt out of place. Being a man in my mid-forties wandering the grounds of a college campus could draw the attention of the campus police. With my record of having been recently released from prison, an encounter with law enforcement could spell trouble.

A familiar laugh caught my attention as Lily emerged from a nearby doorway. Suddenly, the fear of rejection gripped my throat, and I found it hard to breathe, let alone speak. What if she screamed? What if she accused me of stalking her? Could I stand up to her angry glare? It was a risk I had to take. If not, I would never know if we had a shot at becoming a family.

"Lily." I forced her name through strained vocal cords.

She stopped and turned. Like dew, her smile evaporated, scorched by the sun. It was replaced with a condemning stare. "What are *you* doing here?"

I took a deep breath and tried to steady my nerves. "I came because I would like to reconnect with you. You know, spend some time together and ... talk."

"What do you mean you want to reconnect with me?" she snarled.

Her question sliced into my heart like a double-edged sword.

"Haven't you ever wondered about your father or wanted to find out what happened to him?"

Crossing her arms, she held her icy glare. "Mother told me my father died in a car accident before I was born. Nate is my dad now, so what's it to you? You're just the guy who probably murdered my mom."

Lily's words assaulted me like fiery darts. "Correction," I said, lifting a finger. "I'm the guy who was exonerated from being accused of murdering your mom."

I had an ace up my sleeve but I didn't want to use it. But when Lily turned abruptly and began to walk away, I became desperate. "And, I might add, we were once in love."

Lily stopped and glared back at me. "What do you mean you were once in love? My mom said her first husband was a drunk. She never loved him."

Which was probably true, but that didn't blur the fact that I loved her.

I took a deep breath. Tried to control my racing heart and forged ahead. "Look Lily. There are a lot of things your mother didn't tell you, and I'm afraid what she did tell you wasn't all that accurate."

Lily stomped over to a bench and plopped down. Crossing her arms, she huffed. "Okay, you have five minutes. Make it count," her tone acidic.

I stepped closer and took a seat next to her. The bench was cold and hard, much like the last twenty-one years of my life. "Did your mother ever take you to your father's grave?"

"No."

"Did she ever show you a picture of him or mention him?"

"No."

"Doesn't it strike you as odd that in all these years, she never once told you about him?"

"A little," she said, her voice softening and her eyes misted. "I always wondered what he was like ... and if she ever loved him ... and how they met. But whenever I tried to talk to her about it, she'd change the subject or got mad. But what difference does that make to you? Are you some kind of masochist who specializes in ruining people's lives?"

I felt my opportunity slipping between my fingers. "If you'll remember, I *was* the one who saved your life."

Lily's head drooped. "I suppose I owe you my appreciation, but I wouldn't have been in danger in the first place if it weren't for you ... so I guess we're even."

"That's a good point." I conceded. "Would you mind if I show you a picture?"

Lily lifted her head. "I guess not."

As I pulled a wrinkled envelope from my pocket, Lily's eyebrows rose. At least I had her interest.

That was good a good thing.

Slowly, I opened the envelope and slid an old yellowed photograph from its sleeve. The picture had been taken on our wedding day and was the only reminder I had of happier times.

With a slight tremble in her fingers, Lily took the picture. As she studied it, tears welled in her eyes and coursed down her cheeks, making tiny rivulets on her otherwise perfect face.

"This is you and my mom." Her voice broke at the realization.

"Yes. I'm your dad—your real dad." My heart swelled with pride and ached with pain at the same time.

The air between us scintillated with anticipation.

Suddenly, Lily straightened and her eyes grew cold, "I know what this is all about. You just want back into my life for the money. In my whole life, you never once contacted me. You never called me; never sent me a birthday card; never came to see me play in a recital or basketball game. You've been as good as dead; so why don't you just go back to the cave where you've been hiding and leave me alone?"

In that instant, I knew I'd lost her. She was right, of course. But that was only because Monica held a court-ordered restraint over my head. To explain why was too painful, and I understood better than anyone.

Lily let the photograph slip from her fingers. As it fell, the wind blew it across the parking lot. Neither of us moved to retrieve it. For me, it was a closed chapter. For Lily, it was a chapter she had no interest in reading.

With a huff, Lily stood and walked away without looking back; but I couldn't help but notice a slight hesitation as she rested her hand on the doorknob. I wondered if maybe, just maybe, she had one more question for me.

And then she was gone.

Chapter Seventeen

The sudden urge to head to one of my old haunts crawled over me.

I'd been dry for over six years, and it surprised me how strong the desire for a drink was even after all that time. Rather than yield, I followed Ron's instructions ... don't face temptation alone. I stopped at a payphone, dialed a number I'd memorized and waited.

"Ron Wolverton at your service," came a cheery tone. The greeting brought a smile to my face.

Years ago, Ron Wolverton, a former pro-football player and recovering alcoholic, won my confidence and friendship. Prior to my arrest and subsequent incarceration, Ron played a major role in my decision to trust Christ. Since then, Ron stayed in contact with me by written correspondence. It was God's providence that he missed the appointment he had to see me before my scheduled execution, or he might have been caught in the mayhem resulting from the prison riot.

"Ron, Trace here. Can I come over?"

The chair squeaked, and I knew I had Ron's full attention. "Yea, sure, but not at the old location. I'm on staff with Hillcrest Baptist. Have you heard of it? They have an RA outreach ministry, and I'm heading it up."

I pulled the wrapper from a local hamburger joint out of a trash can prepared to jot down the address. "I'm ready, give me the address." I scribbled it down. "Okay, got it. I'll see you in a few minutes."

"Hold on. Let me check my schedule." A minute later, he came back. "I've cleared my schedule. I can't wait to see you."

I hung up already feeling the tentacles of temptation starting to relax their grip but I knew how weak I was. I needed an accountability partner, one who'd walked in my shoes and come through victorious.

After checking the bus routes, I took the next bus to the outskirts of Sacramento. It dropped me off a block from the church and I walked the rest of the way. The building occupied a large piece of property and showed signs of recent construction. Following the signs to the church office, I entered and scanned the lobby. Soft, melodious music emanated from speakers situated in the ceiling. The foyer itself was spacious and well-appointed giving me the feeling I was welcome to sit and stay a while.

Recent renovations and upgrades were evident, from the new carpet smell to the fresh coat of paint unsullied by little hands. I pushed deeper along the tiled floor until I reached a glass-enclosed office where a prim secretary sat reading a book.

It had been a long time since I'd been in church. My obligatory visit with Monica on Christmas or Easter never left a lasting impression. This was different. I was here because this was where I could find God.

"May I help you?" the secretary's cheery tone echoed from behind the glass.

"Yes, I'm here to see Ron Wolverton."

"Yes, Pastor Ron told me he was expecting you." Standing, she came around her desk. "Follow me. These halls can get a little confusing if you've not been here before."

I felt a slight tinge of guilt, but quickly let it pass.

"Well, I am somewhat new to the area. I mean, I used to live here, but I've been away for a number of years." I found myself blathering on. I chalked it up to nerves.

I was glad for the escort, however. There were more halls and intersections than any prison I'd ever seen. Finally, the young twentyish guide reached a door marked "Outreach Minister" and knocked.

"Enter to learn, go forth to serve," came a man's booming voice.

The secretary smiled at his welcome. "He says that to everyone," she whispered as she pushed the door open.

Ron stood and came around his cluttered desk.

"Trace, how in heaven are you?" he asked, pulling me into a huge bear hug.

I allowed myself to be enfolded, feeling the warmth of true friendship. After a moment, the large man released his hold and stepped back.

"Well, since I never made it there, maybe the better question should be; how on earth am I?" I said, smiling back at my friend. "I must say, I'm … I'm … struggling."

Ron's deep brown eyes softened. Nodding to the secretary, he said, "That will be all, Miss Shelley. Hold my calls, this may take a while."

She smiled and backed away, letting the door softly close behind her.

Retaking his seat, Ron gave me his full attention. "A lot of people were praying for you. Not just for your release, but that you would finish well no matter the outcome."

I slouched into a color-coordinated chair across from my friend. "If it weren't for Rose Beretta, things would have turned out quite differently. Now that I'm out, I find the old tendencies beckoning me."

Ron nodded knowingly. It was not the first time he'd heard that confession, and it wouldn't be the last. "I'm here for you, you know that buddy?"

I nodded. "Yeah, I just need someone to talk to."

"I'm all ears. What's got those old demons stirred up?"

For the next forty-five minutes, I unpacked most of what had happened in the prison riot and my escape. Actually, it was Lily's rejection that nearly sent me careening over the edge.

Ron listened with the interest of a good friend. Finally, after I'd unburdened myself, he sat back and released a low whistle. "That's quite a load to bear in just one week. Let's pray over these issues then get a bite to eat. I am confident God will give you some insight as to how to proceed with your daughter."

I took a cleansing breath.

The idea of a free meal and someone to talk to appealed to me.

Standing, Ron came around his desk, took a seat next to me and bowed his head. His prayer was not eloquent, just a simple man with a simple request. In layman's terms, he laid out the need for me to reconnect with Lily, that God would soften her rebel heart and that He would teach me how to love her. As to the matter of finding my wife's killer, he simply reminded me that vengeance belonged to the Lord, that He would repay the evil doer in His good time. When he finished, I felt the burden lift.

"Now let's grab a bite. I've got an RA meeting in an hour, so we can't go too far."

"We'll need to take your car. I got here using public transportation, and I'll probably need a ride home. My car was in the garage when I was arrested and I haven't had the money to pay off the garage," I quipped as we strolled to the parking lot.

"Okay, on one condition, that you stay for the meeting. I think it will do you a lot of good."

Nodding, I smiled. "That sounds like good advice. I don't need to be alone tonight."

Chapter Eighteen

I checked and rechecked the departing flight schedule as I waited for my flight to Atlanta, Georgia to be called.

This trip was item number two on my to-do list. I wanted to meet my former partner's widow. Jimmy Barlow and I trained together and were assigned to the same unit upon graduation. We worked our way up through the ranks and he was my best friend and drinking buddy. For five years, we were nearly inseparable. During that time, we'd solved many of the toughest cases in and around Sacramento.

Two years into my incarceration, Jimmy's car was found in the bottom of a ravine. Recent heavy rains had washed away a large section of the road sending him to his death. Although no body was recovered, his death was listed as natural causes and filed away. It left his widow with a wall of trophies and a pile of debt.

Due to a prior commitment with the death sentence, I missed his funeral and I wanted to offer my condolences. That and ask Susan Barlow a few questions. I hoped they wouldn't upset her too much. My call hadn't been very encouraging.

The drive from the Hartsfield-Jackson Atlanta International Airport took longer than I'd expected, but it was a dazzling spring day in Georgia which meant a heavy concentration of pollen. For months, everything that didn't move had been covered with a thin layer of yellow. Fortunately, June brought with it the rainy season which cleared the air and washed the pollen into the lakes scattered around the region. With my window down, I let the warm air glide over my bare arm.

$$$

"Hello, Susan."

She swung the door open and pulled me into a tight squeeze. "Hi, Trace. It's so good to see you. Please, come in." Susan's welcome was as natural as sitting at my own dinner table. The kindness in her voice and warm glow in her eyes let me know my concerns were unfounded.

"May I get you something to drink?" Her body movement told me 'no' was not an option.

"Yes, please."

She disappeared into the kitchen and soon returned with a sturdy mug of iced tea. The doubly sweet mixture of half tea and half lemonade took my palate by storm.

"Umm, what is it?"

Her face brightened into a broad smile. "It's an Arnold Palmer. Like it?"

I took another swig and peered over the rim of the Kerr jar. "They should bottle it and patent its ingredients."

She nodded and handed me the empty can. "They have."

I studied the label but found the print too small to read. Setting it aside, I looked at Susan, who waited expectantly. In my phone call to her a few days ago I warned her I had many unanswered questions. Questions only she had the answers to.

The lines around her eyes showed the strain she bore. Maybe by sharing it, it would make it easier. Kinda like me sharing my burden with Ron. I hoped so.

"It's too bad you weren't able to come to Jim's funeral," she said. "You would have liked it."

I nodded. "I read about it in the paper." I finished my tea and set the jar on the table. "I understand he died in the line of duty."

"Duty!" she said it as if it were a dirty word. "It wasn't 'duty.' It was devotion. That man lived for the truth and wouldn't sleep until he found it. It didn't matter where it took him or what it cost him. You know it as well as I do. In this case, it cost him ..." She let her voice trail off.

I searched her face looking for signs of anger or bitterness. There was none. She was simply a lonely, tired soul.

"That was Jimmy. And that was me. Look what it cost us." I paused, dreading my next question. "Do you have any idea what he was working on?"

She twisted a dish towel nervously in her hands and stared at the floor. "After you were incarcerated, he refused to take on another partner ... said breaking in one was enough." A smile creased her eyes. "Since then, he worked alone. It was as if he were driven ... working twice as hard." She laughed nervously. "I think he was trying to pull your weight as well as his." She paused and held my gaze. "You know, he never believed you murdered Monica."

"I appreciate his confidence in me. There were times when I even doubted myself. Did he ever mention anything or leave any notes to indicate he was on to something?"

With effort, Susan rose to her feet … as if she had known I would ask. She stepped to an old roll-top desk, turned a rusty key, and raised the lid. She pulled out a drawer and removed a stack of papers tied with a string. Its long wait was nearly over. With great care, she lifted the bundle and handed it to me as if it was something sacred, and maybe it was. These were the last thoughts her husband had, and she cherished them, guarded them, shielded them from unworthy eyes.

"The department was quite insistent that I turn over all of Jimmy's case notes. I gave them all the old stuff, the closed files and dead ends. But the stuff he was working on after hours, I kept here, in this desk. Somehow I knew in my heart you would come looking for them. He was doing his own investigating on the side when his car—" her voice faltered, and she brushed aside a single tear. Then she handed me a yellowed envelope. "I had a feeling these might come in handy someday." An impish twinkle flickered in her eyes.

For a moment, I just held the bundle. For the first time since my release, I felt a sense of purpose. "I feel like Jimmy is trying to reach out to me through these," I said through emotionally clogged vocal cords. "Trying to point me to my wife's killer. At least I hope so."

Retaking her seat, Susan continued, "Trace, you don't know how many times I prayed for you and Jimmy. You won't find lasting peace in that stack of papers or in a bottle either. The only place you'll find peace is in the person of Jesus Christ. My only regret is that Jimmy didn't make his peace with God before he—" her throat closed and she choked back a sob.

I looked down at the envelope. My fingers trembled slightly as I peeled back the flap and slid the pages out. They were yellowed, dog-eared, handwritten notes—the last efforts of my closest friend to prove my innocence. However, they only contained names, dates, times, and statements. They possessed no lasting peace, nor could they.

"You're right, Susan. If it weren't for Jesus, I wouldn't have made it through six years of hell on earth or faced death with confidence. Thank you for your prayers."

After a long pause, I stood and drew her into a warm embrace and held her tight. Releasing her I asked. "Say, Susan, do you have another one of those cans of tea?"

She smiled as if she'd half expected the request. "Here," she said, handing me the remaining cans. "Do you think they'll let you carry them on the flight back?"

"They will."

"Oh! Why? Because you're some hot-shot detective?"

"Nope, because I'll be smuggling them in my bladder." I patted my stomach.

She reached out and gave me another hug. "Same old Trace ... the guy with the biggest bladder in the world. Don't be a stranger. I'm just a Red-Eye away."

I took a small step toward the door and paused. "Any thought of moving back?"

She shook her head. "Too many memories. I moved here to take care of my grandkids. Now that they're grown, I'm waiting on the great-grandkids."

$$\$\$\$$

The flight back to Sacramento was excruciatingly slow, considering the volume of information and tea I'd consumed.

By the time I entered my extended-stay apartment, I was exhausted. But I was certain of one thing. Jimmy died because he'd gotten too close to the truth. Now it was my turn to pick up on Jimmy's unfinished work and not get killed in the process.

$$\$\$\$$

After a long flight and getting to bed around midnight, the last thing I wanted was to be awakened by a telephone.

That was not to be.

The source of the annoyance sat cradled on the nightstand next to the bed. I rolled over and pulled the covers over my head, hoping the impertinent device would stop.

It didn't.

Frustrated, I threw the sheets back and reached for the phone, missed it, and sent it bouncing to the floor. By the time I'd found it and picked it up, the ringing had stopped.

"Sleep is impossible now," I muttered.

Straining through bleary eyes, I looked at the clock. Two a.m. screamed back at me. For a moment, I considered hitting the redial when the decision was made for me.

I cleared my throat and coughed out a muddled, "Hello?"

"Congratulations on getting a second lap around the track. Not many of us do, you know." The sultry voice was partially familiar.

"Who is this? Is this some kind of joke?"

A deep chuckle emanated across the airwaves. "Why Trace, I'm offended. Don't you recognize my voice? It's me, Cami. Remember?"

The vision of her face flashed before my eyes. "Oh, yes, Cami. Good to hear from you," I lied. "Why the late-night call?"

Wild music blared in the background and I knew she wasn't in a revival meeting.

Her voice came close to the phone, and she whispered, "Sorry, I forgot about the time change."

Time change? I'd totally forgotten about that. Should I move the clock forward or backward?

It didn't matter now.

"Can we talk?" Cami continued. "I mean, not like this. Can we meet somewhere, say tomorrow at noon?"

My mind raced. W*hy, after all these years, would a high-class gal like Cami Stetson want to meet with me, an* *ex-con?* Though innocent, the stigma of being on death-row still followed me like a ball and chain.

"Yeah sure. Where do you want to meet?"

Not missing a beat, she said, "There's a park just down the street from where you're staying. I'll meet you there at noon sharp."

I sat straight up in bed. I'd only been out of prison a week and was staying in an Extended-Stay motel. How she found me was a mystery.

"A park? How'd you know where I was staying?"

Click!

I stared at the phone, wondering what I'd gotten myself into.

Chapter Nineteen

"Trace O'Reilly? Is that you?"

I lifted the ball cap, which I'd pulled down to cover my eyes to block the sun. Having drifted off while waiting for Cami, I cracked open an eye and found myself staring at a large black lab. On the other end of a heavy tether was its owner … Cami Stetson.

"You look so," she paused as if trying to choose the right word, "different."

Sitting upright on the park bench, I peered up at her. "Yeah, prison will do that to ya. They had me on a strict diet. Plus, they had a killer exit plan." I palmed my bleary eyes and stifled back a yawn. "I guess I fell asleep waiting for you. What took you so long?"

She plopped down next to me. Her freshly applied cologne waved over me like an incoming sea breeze. "Late night too hmm?"

"No, long flight and an annoying phone call."

Cami ignored the barb. "I have a job, you know."

"Do you own a watch?"

"Hey, that's not fair. I remember a few late-night calls from a hot-shot detective, and I never got testy." She sounded almost hurt.

I knew better.

Wag, the black lab tugged at the end of the leash and she stood. "Let's walk."

I matched strides with her. "It's been a long time, why the sudden urgency?" I asked. It had been over eight years since we broke up. Did she want to get back together? Did she still love me? Did I still love her?

She took my hand and pulled me along as she tried to keep up with her dog. "You were a bit incommunicado there for a while."

I jammed my free hand in my pocket. "You could have written. After all, we were together for two years. It wasn't that bad, was it?"

She sighed, "Well no, not at first, but you have to admit, you weren't yourself when you were on a drinking binge."

I winched at the memory; the pain I'd caused her, the pain I'd caused Monica."

"So why did you act like you didn't know me when we were at Sanchez's birthday party?"

She shrugged. "Oh I don't know, with you trying to break up the Beretta crime-ring, I thought it best to keep my distance. Plus, with your ex lurking around, well, it wouldn't have been a pretty sight. Who knows, I might have tossed her down the steps. Instead, someone else got to her first."

"So you think it was intentional? I mean Monica; you think someone actually killed her?"

"You got it."

"Well, I for sure didn't do it."

"That only leaves a dozen others," Cami said counting on her fingers.

"And what about Nate? Don't you trust Nate's motives?"

Cami coughed out a laugh. "Motives? I don't trust anyone's motives, and neither should you."

The confession brought me little comfort. "So why did you call me?"

Cami stepped behind the trunk of an ancient oak tree, glanced around, then lowered her voice. "I'm being followed. My phone's been tapped, and I think someone's hacked into my computer."

Leaning against the tree, I felt its rough bark. I liked having something solid to lean on. "I'm not surprised. What do you think they're looking for?"

She shook her head. A light breeze ruffled her short-cropped hair, and she rubbed her arms with her hand to brush away the chill. "You know I work for Rafael Sanchez, don't you? He's the governor now."

"Yeah, he signed my reprieve. Ever since he was elected as governor, he's been itching for a shot at the White House." I said, avoiding eye contact.

"Did you know he's about to make a big announcement?"

"Yes! I'm not without my sources. So what's the big deal?"

Cami shifted uncomfortably as if not wanting to tell all too soon. "The governor's got a lot of baggage if you know what I mean."

I relaxed my stance and waited. "I thought he'd been checked out by the FBI, CIA, and every other agency with the TLA, the three-lettered acronyms."

She stepped away from the tree, found a park bench and plopped down. Patting the space next to her, she invited me to sit. "I know things, things that some people would pay a lot to get their hands on."

"Or kill for?"

She nodded. "That too."

I let out a low whistle. "So who do you think is snooping around?"

Her eyes shifted left and right. Lowering her voice conspiratorially, she whispered, Nate Peterson."

I wasn't surprised. "He's a very influential attorney with lots of friends and a lot of ambition. Why am I not surprised that he's sniffing around? But I can't go investigating the state's public defender. What would that look like? Anyway, I'm just now trying to put my life back together. Society hasn't been very kind to me recently."

She let out a nervous laugh. "Yes, but you've got, like tons of connections. You know people. Maybe you could do a little, uh, research of your own. Find something I could use to make Nate back off."

"How do you know it's Nate? It could be anyone."

"Maybe, but you're the detective. You have a nose for these things."

"Correction, I was a detective. Now I'm just an unemployed gum-shoe."

Her eyelids lowered and she chuckled. "You know what I meant. Anyway, you still remember how to kick over a few rocks. Don't you? Who knows, you might find something."

"You know me too well. I keep forgetting that we were together for two years."

She bit her lower lip. "Yeah, two years in which you proved yourself to be the best detective in the department."

I smirked. "And how many detectives have you known, anyway?"

"You'd be surprised; I work for the governor, remember?"

"What kind of stuff do you want me to get on Nate?"

Finger to her chin, she paused. "Oh, just common stuff, like why is Lily seeing a psychologist? And what will happen to the million dollars in a private trust if she doesn't live to see her twenty-first birthday. Which, I might add, is in a few weeks."

We locked eyes. "Now there's a motive to kill for. Where do I start?"

"You could start by reviewing the notes and files from the case."

I stood and glanced down at her. "Any chance we could, uh, pick up where we left off?"

My question came from too many nights alone and I regretted it the moment I said it. Since we'd split up, I'd changed a lot. I'd given my life to Christ, kicked the drinking habit and refocused my priorities. I wasn't the man I used to be and I certainly wasn't in the market for a new relationship. On the other hand, if Cami was willing, well ...

Thankfully, her shoulders rose and fell slightly saving the embarrassment of an explanation. "No, I don't think so."

Reaching into her purse, she pulled out an envelope and handed it to me. "Here, take this. It will help you get started. Rent yourself a decent apartment, get some better clothes, and buy a car. You'll need it."

Fingering the envelope, I peered into her eyes. They pulled me in and I knew the flame we'd shared hadn't gone completely out. "Where'd you get this stack of money?"

A quizzical look shadowed her alluring features. "I've been saving it, so be thankful. I could have retired early on that." With a quick jerk of the leash, she turned and began jogging with Wag leading the way.

"How can I reach you, if I find anything?" I called after her.

"It's easy. I go wherever the governor goes."

Chapter Twenty

L ily stepped into the examination room.

It was her semi-annual check-up and she dreaded it.

The doctor, an expert in the field of post-traumatic stress disorder, followed his routine as he had for the last six years.

Using an ophthalmoscope, he peered into her eyes to see if there was any change. Satisfied that he saw none, he checked her reflexes and balance. He had her repeat a set of words and letters backward. She followed his instructions without complaint. Pulling a clean sheet of paper from his desk, he placed it on a work table and handed her a pencil.

"Now Lily, I am going to count backward, and when I snap my fingers, you will go to sleep. Okay?"

She nodded her assent.

"10, 9, 8, 7, 6, 4, 3, 2, 1"

Snap!

Lily sat unblinking.

"Good, now I'm going to leave you here alone and I want you to draw a picture of whatever you see. When you're finished, I'll return and give you a big bowl of double chocolate ice cream. Okay?"

Fifteen minutes later, the doctor returned, with a large bowl held above his head. He snapped his fingers, and Lily blinked.

"There now, that wasn't so bad after all. Was it?"

She sat, glaring at him. "You know I don't like ice cream, especially chocolate. Why did you trick me?"

The doctor allowed a slight laugh to clear his throat. "Sorry, it's all part of the test to see if you were really under the influence of hypnosis."

"And?" her bitterness seeped through the single word.

"And despite my best efforts … you weren't."

"So who tricked who?" she asked, handing him her drawing.

He studied the stick figures with interest. They were exactly the same as they were the last time.

The doctor stood and paced the floor, his hands folded behind his back. "Have you been sleeping well, Miss Lily?"

A moment of silence passed. Only the ticking of the clock on the wall marked the passage of time. She let out a weak sigh. "I've been having dreams." She released a nervous laugh, "More like nightmares."

The doctor's eyebrows rose. "Oh? And when did they start?" he probed.

She stared out the window at the little sparrow that had landed on the ledge. Wishing she could sprout wings, she stood and neared the glass. "I didn't start having them until that evil man showed up."

"If you're referring to Mr. O'Reilly, I can understand. It must have been quite a shock."

Lily ground her teeth at his saccharine tone.

"Is there anything else you'd like to say?"

She remained motionless, staring at the bird. Unmoving.

"Well, thank you, Miss Lily, I believe that concludes our little game."

She turned to leave. As she reached for the doorknob, he said, "Oh, Lily, I forgot to mention one thing."

Cocking her head, she asked, "And what would that be?"

"What number did I miss?"

Lily stood, hand on the knob. Her eyes wide as a stop-watch. "You didn't miss any number," she said, without emotion.

"5"

Lily snapped to life. "Doctor, is it time for our visit?" a bright smile painted her lovely features.

"No Lily. I'm afraid something's come up, and I'll have to postpone it for another time. You run along now and have a happy twenty-first birthday."

She smiled and scampered from the examination room.

$$\$\$\$$$

Nate smiled at Lily as she left the examination room.

He squeezed passed her and glanced at the doctor.

Closing the door behind him, he took a seat across from the elderly man and waited for the report.

"I don't know what else to tell you, Mr. Peterson. Lily is still suffering from a type of post-traumatic stress syndrome."

"How long will it last, Doc?"

"There's no telling. She may never recover. One thing's for sure. She won't come out of it until she is good and ready," the elderly gentleman said, leaning back in his chair.

Nate stood and ran his fingers through his thinning hair. "Isn't there something you can do?"

The doctor lifted a prescription pad, scribbled a note, and tore it off. "Here, this might help, but I gotta tell ya, time heals better than meds. Oh, by the way, she's having dreams again."

The word struck Nate like a punch in the gut. "I was afraid of that."

"Here's her latest art work." He handed Nate the picture. He grimaced, folded it, and stuck it in his coat pocket.

"In two weeks, Lily will be twenty-one. After that ... we won't be back."

The doctor nodded knowingly. "I understand, but if she ever wants to talk, I'll be more than happy to listen."

Chapter Twenty-One

Taking Cami's advice, I rented a two-room apartment, bought a car, a vintage Renault, and applied for a private investigator's license.

While I waited for the state to approve my application, I resorted to a local coffee shop where I listened to classical music, drank copious amounts of the best blend money could buy, and reviewed Jimmy's notes. In time, I became convinced there was a connection between Sanchez and Luciano. It was probably what got him killed. Except for the name Guillermo popping up and a few obscure addresses, it provided little to go on. As far as helping me with the investigation, I needed to dig deeper—I just hoped it didn't get me killed too.

I dreaded my next move but made the trip downtown to meet with my former boss. Stepping into the Sacramento Police Department headquarters was like a bad dream ... only worse.

Not much had changed. It still smelled of sweat, stale coffee and overworked police officers. The crowd noise dipped only slightly as I entered, then returned to its frustratingly high level.

"Well looky here, if it ain't the former Detective Trace O'Reilly, fresh from death row," the police chief said, sarcasm seeping from every pore. "Tell me, Mr. O'Reilly, did you catch public enemy number one while doing all that undercover work?" His snarky remark scraped like sandpaper.

I felt streaks of anger creep up my neck like vines. *Lord, give me grace not to say something I'll regret.*

I stepped back and took a breath. "No, it was just about like working in the detective division. Some people you can trust and some you can't." I made a quick about-face and headed for the records department.

"Don't think you're going to get any better welcome down in records, dude," the chief called after me.

"Dude," I shot back. "Just because you're from California, doesn't mean you have to talk like a beach bum."

A few police officers snickered at my comment.

$$$

After several attempts at gaining access to the police files and failing, I finally gave up and headed to the Court House.

I applied for the court records under the Freedom of Information Act and was met with a stack of paperwork. I knew by the time I got through it, they'd have another stack for me to fill out. "They called it stonewalling," I muttered.

After developing hand cramps from signing the reams of papers, I finally handed them to the clerk. The elderly man peeked at me through coke-bottle bottom glasses. I felt like I was a schoolboy turning in a writing assignment. He gave the sheets a cursory look and disappeared deeper into the records department.

I waited, rubbing my hand.

A few minutes later, he returned.

"Here is what we have," the clerk said.

An hour later, all I had for my trouble was a transcript of the court proceedings … nothing more; no addendums, no depositions or standard of proof.

"Looks like a lynching, if you ask me," I said after skimming the last sheet of paper. I handed the folder back to the clerk who'd been eyeing me suspiciously. "Thanks for your trouble."

"No problemo." His lips formed a straight line.

Getting back in my car, I released a frustrated breath. "That was a waste of time. I'm no closer to solving this than I was when I started." I cranked the engine and it sputtered to life. While I let the heater warm up the interior, I flipped through my notes. "Let's see, no luck at the precinct, not much at the courthouse; next, a background check on my old buddy, Nate. I'll check his credit scores, spending habits, bars he frequents, ask a few questions and see what I can come up with. If worse comes to worse, I can always pay him a visit and see if I can rattle him."

It was doubtful.

Knowing a search warrant was out of the question, I had few options. The straight in approach would probably be the best, but the least likely to produce any results. No doubt it would alert him that I was investigating him, I had to admit. On the other hand, breaking into his house is not only illegal, but it would get me thrown back in the slammer. That was an option I would really like to avoid.

Yes, sirree.

As I considered my options, an idea popped into my head. Maybe I could go in under the guise of a utility worker.

My phone chirped, and I pulled it from its pouch. I felt the tension in my face relax into a smile as Cami's name appeared on the caller ID.

"Hey, Cami, what's up?"

"Trace, have you been listening to the news?"

"No, why?"

"My boss, the governor just won the party's nomination for the presidency."

I had been so busy; I'd totally missed the presidential convention which took place in July. Now that Sanchez was officially running for office, I figured I'd better start. "Well, I guess congratulations are in order. You're going to Washington."

"Nope, not going to happen, not without a miracle."

"Why's that?"

"He's got so much baggage I'm surprised he even got the nomination. Plus, he's exhibiting some strange behavior."

"Strange in what way?"

Her tone softened. "I'm sorry, I shouldn't have said that. Forget I even brought it up. I'm just tired and I haven't even started."

I heard the frustration seeping through the connection. The urge to reach through the phone and hold her was palpable.

"How about you, Trace? Have you made any progress?"

"Yeah, I found out how loyal or greedy the police and the court system are. I've hit a brick wall. I've been sitting here considering my options—"

"You need to get into Nate's house. Rumor has it, he's hiding a treasure trove of info about your case."

My heart rate ratcheted up a notch. "I had a feeling he was hiding something. But I couldn't break into his house, not without a police escort and a warrant. Got any suggestions?"

Silence filled the connection.

"Cami, are you there?"

"Yeah, I was just thinking."

"And?"

"Nate takes Lily to a shrink every six months. As a matter of fact, I have it on good authority that's where they are now."

"What's his address? Maybe I could swing by and scope out his house."

Cami rattled it off. "I'm not far. I'll meet you there in fifteen minutes."

Taken aback, I wondered if this was a setup. "Whoa, slow down. You're not thinking what I'm thinking you're thinking … are you? I'm not willing to risk jail for a petty break-in." Visions of prison bars flashed in front of my eyes.

"We don't have to break in. I have a snitch who told me where he keeps his files. We can do it without breaking in."

"But, but, but—"

The call ended.

I took a hard swallow and stared at the inert device.

What am I getting myself into?

Exactly fifteen minutes later, I parked my Renault across the street from Peterson's house and watched a dark-green BMW roll to a stop at the end of the block. A tall, well-shaped woman in a professional suit stepped out and walked briskly in my direction.

A bright, optimistic sun highlighted her hair, making her look like a model prancing down the runway.

Smiling at the sight, I unfolded myself from my car and met her at the mailbox. Its rusty flap hung lazily open like a largemouth bass.

"What's your grand plan?" I asked, eyeing her with admiration.

"Don't gawk, it makes me nervous." She turned her back to me. "You're still staring."

"I'm sure by now you're used to it."

"What's that supposed to mean?"

"Just look at you. You're the governor's spokesperson. He's a candidate, and you go where he goes. Besides, you're dressed to the nines, you keep yourself in great shape, and you have a professional hair and makeup artist making you camera ready—"

"I'll have you know I do my own hair and face, thank you very much, but I don't want my looks to distract you."

"Don't worry… it won't." I couldn't help the smile which played on my lips.

"What's that supposed to mean?"

Before I could answer, the neighbor's dog raced across the yard barking wildly at the intruders. Grabbing a stick from the yard, I stepped between Cami and the belligerent dog.

"Here boy, fetch." I tossed it as far as I could. The dog turned and scampered after the stick.

Sighing relief, she watched in amazement. "Nice move."

I feigned dusting off my hands. "That should keep the mutt occupied for a while. Let's hurry."

The deserted street and empty houses surrounding the Peterson home didn't relieve the jitters I was feeling in my gut. Neither did the open barn type garage which sat behind Peterson's home.

Taking care not to trip, we made our way to the rickety steps and into the upper attic. A loose board shifted and she let out a stifled cry. I grabbed her hand to support her. Surprisingly, her fingers closed around mine. Though icy with excited energy, her hand felt good to touch. She didn't pull back and that felt good too.

Light from the front window filtered in giving them enough illumination to see ahead.

With care, she crossed the room to a set of filing cabinets. She pulled. "Shoot, they're locked."

"What'd you think?" Giving the handle a quick jerk, the drawer popped open. "This gives new meaning to the open records act," I said, a smug grin tugged at the corners of my mouth.

Cami stared at the organized files. "I should hire him to do my filing. Just look at these, they're even alphabetical."

"Looks like we found the missing files," I whispered. I pulled the first file folder out and dropped it on a work table. Dust curled up in ever widening-circles causing her to sneeze.

"God bless you," I said, not looking up.

"Yeah right, I'm sure He's going to bless us for snooping in someone's private cache of stolen court documents."

"You know we can't use these in court. We've obtained this evidence illegally."

"Yes, I know, but maybe you can use it to lead you to the truth anyway."

I nodded and pulled out my cell phone. "There's not enough time to read all this stuff. Help me and let's get this over before they return," I said as I snapped the first of a dozen pictures.

Within a short time, we'd made a digital copy of all the important records.

"There, now let's put these back in the file and get out of here. Nate could return at any time," Cami said.

A minute later, we slipped down the stairs and crossed the yard, heading for our cars. "Shoot me your images, will ya, Cami? I'll print them out and begin to piece them together."

She nodded and tossed me her phone. "Here, I have another one, good luck." Turning, she began to hike back to her car.

"Any chance we could get together for dinner?" I yelled.

A wave of her hand was all I got.

Feeling rejected, I sucked in a breath and let it out slowly. As I got in my car, my phone vibrated with a text.

thkn abt it.

Smiling, I cranked the engine.

As I pulled away from the curb, movement caught my eye. I glanced over my shoulder. *Did that curtain move? Was someone home? Nah, it couldn't be.*

Chapter Twenty-Two

"How did it go at the doctor's visit," Nelson asked as Lily and his brother entered the house.

Lily ignored the question. "I'm not feeling so well. So if it's all the same to you, I'm going upstairs and take a nap."

Nate touched her shoulder lightly. "Can I get you something? A ginger ale?"

"Nah."

She plodded toward the stairs, steadied herself and continued.

Nelson's eyes followed her until she was out of sight.

Tossing Lily's most recent artwork on the table, Nate released a frustrated breath. "Frankly, I'm worried."

Nelson dragged his eyes from the stairs. Nelson, Nate's twin brother, had taken up residence with him. After losing his malpractice suit to Monica, which left him bankrupt, he spent several more years in prison for operating an illegal practice. For the last ten years, he'd been in and out of alcohol and drug treatment centers. It was only recently that he'd gotten his life under control. However, his private women's clinic on the seedy side of town was the center of much controversy and a thorn in the side of his brother.

Nelson glanced up from the picture. "How so?"

"This picture — there's a slight difference from the others."

Snatching it from his hand, Nelson stared at it. "I don't see anything different."

Nate held it to the light, "Yes, there it is. She's a smart girl. Those marks on the other side are not mistakes, they're intentional. When you hold it up, it makes a perfect picture. I think she's coming out of her trauma. I think she's remembering."

Nelson slammed his palm on the table making the silverware jump. "But I don't want her to remember. Why do you think I've kept my mouth shut all these years? She's not supposed to remember anything." He paused to regain his composure. "It's too painful, I mean, seeing her mother fall to her death. She'll be scarred for life."

Straightening, he began pacing the floor. "She's already scarred. The question is, to what extent? She's so young, so full of life. I just hate to see her living in fear, constantly looking over her shoulder. Isn't there anything we can do to help her?" Nelson asked, folding the paper.

Nate glanced upward as if he could see through the ceiling. "I'll see what I can do." He took a step toward the back door.

"Oh, and by the way Nate, you had visitors today."

"Visitors? What kind of visitors?"

Nelson came around the table and lowered his voice as if Lily could hear. "The nosy kind."

"Well why didn't you stop them, you fool?"

"For the same reason I'm staying here, to keep a low profile. My clinic is already raising a stink. If I called the police, they'd had to fill out a report and my name would appear on it. I can't have that kind of scrutiny, not yet."

Nate let out a curse. "Did they find anything?

"How should I know. They weren't here that long."

"Do you know who they were?" Nate asked, his voice rising.

"No," he lied, "like I said, they weren't there that long.

"There? There, where?" his voice turning frantic.

"They went around back. I think they were checking out your barn—"

"My barn—" the phone rang, cutting him off. He snatched it up and barked a curt greeting. "Okay, I'll be there in twenty minutes."

Looking at Nelson, he huffed. "If they come back, call me, then call the police."

Nelson nodded sullenly. "Sure thing, but I doubt they'll be back."

"Do it anyway," Nate spat, then turned to leave.

Nelson watched his brother climb into his late-model sedan and drive off. Only after he was sure his brother would not return, did he ascend the stairs and peek in on Lily.

She was sleeping.

That was good.

Keeping the door open by a crack, he stood stock still. And stared.

Chapter Twenty-Three

B y the time I got back to my apartment, I had more questions than answers.

Why were the police stonewalling me? What did Cami know? And how did the DA get his hands on all those files and not get caught?

I placed the Sim-card into my computer and began to scan the pages of notes Cami and I had taken. My stomach knotted when I opened the file bearing the name State versus Trace O'Reilly. A slight tremor ran through my fingers as I began sifting through the facts.

"Let's see now." My habit of talking to myself had lodged itself so deeply in my psyche that I barely heard myself speaking. "They placed Monica's time of death sometime between 11:00 p.m. and 11:45. We know that because Carnes, the Butler, reported finding her around 11:30." Using a dry-erase marker, I wrote the time on a white-board I'd placed in the living room. Then I wrote the butler's name and connected the two circles with a line.

"And the maid, what's her name?" I looked through the notes, "Hmm, no name. The maid left the kitchen, passed by the stairs around the same time and found the body."

Another circle.

Another line.

Since I memorized the floor plan of the mansion, I drew it in a different color. Then I meticulously placed all the principal suspects in the locations they claimed to be in at the time of the murder. I placed myself in my room and wrote 10:50 p.m. with the words - 'heard voices.' Then I drew two stick figures in the men's den with an arrow to a circle around Luciano and Sanchez.

"I'd love to have been a fly on the wall and heard what went on between those two," I whispered.

Like pawns on a chessboard, I placed Cami and the rest of the ladies in the lounge, and Nate and the men in the game room with the time 11:00-+ behind it.

"Okay now, let's review—"

Someone pounded on my door sending my heart skipping. The heavy knocking rattled the door on its rickety hinges. It wasn't the best hotel in the neighborhood, but it was all I could afford. By the sound of it, I figured it was some massive policeman here to arrest me for driving a clunker. I wiped my sweaty palms on my jean pants and crossed the room. With my heart in my throat, I flung the door open.

Chapter Twenty-Four

C ami, dressed in tight jeans and a loose cowl necked sweater, stood outside with a pizza box in one hand and a six-pack of soda in the other.

"Well, are you going to make me stand here in the cold or are you going to invite me in?" Her voice carried a playful tone.

Giving her a grand bow, I ushered her in and closed the door. Only then did I realize she had company. Her black lab pranced into the living room as if he owned the place.

She breezed into the kitchen and tossed the pizza box on the counter. It slid, knocking over the salt shaker. Then she handed me a cold drink.

"Hungry?"

My breathing slowed and I returned her smile. "Famished, I see you brought your dog."

Cami knelt down and massaged the dog's face. "Wag, his name is Wag, and yes, I don't go anywhere without my little poochy," she said with an impudent face. Wag jumped on my second-hand couch and curled in a tight circle.

Looking at the smaller version of the Hound of the Baskervilles, I considered shoving his fanny off my couch, but decided against it.

"If I were you, Trace, I'd avoid making any quick moves around him."

Cami must have read my mind.

I felt like my house had just been invaded. I just hoped he wasn't carrying any ticks or flees.

"Well, why don't you make yourself at home," I said dejectedly.

Wag offered me an ample yawn.

"Oh, he'll be fine, Trace. If you want him to move, all you need to do is push him out of the way."

"Yeah, and come back with a nub." I turned back and caught her giving me an appreciative once over. The corners of her lips lilted and I wondered what she thought of me. I'd taken up jogging to counter my coffee interests. So I knew I was in much better shape than before my stint in prison. "So how'd you break free from Sanchez, anyway?"

She plopped down on one of two bar stools. "He's in a photo-shoot all day, and he sent me to pack for a whirl-wind trip around the state. We leave in the morning. So you and I have a lot to do in the next few hours." She snatched a slice of pizza and walked to the white-board and studied it.

After taking a bite, she said out of the corner of her mouth, "You've got that all wrong," pointing at my timeline.

I pinched my eyes shut and offered up a quick prayer of thanks. With interest growing, I stepped next to her, a large slice of pizza in my hand. Her freshly applied cologne stole my attention, temporarily replacing my appetite for food. Mechanically, I took a bite, chewed, and swallowed. Before I knew it, the slice was gone. I blinked away the memories of the two of us sitting together in a theater or restaurant and tried to focus on what she was saying. With a grand stroke, she transformed my timeline.

"So when did you get religion?"

I suppressed a smile at the poorly phrased question. "I didn't get religion. After you and I split up, I hit rock bottom. My drinking got out of hand, and I had nowhere to turn. I ended up at a drug and alcohol rehab center where I met this guy named Ron Wolverton. Man, was he tough, but fair. After I got dried out, he told me how I could have lasting peace, something I couldn't get from a bottle. I finally understood who Jesus really is, what He did for me. I gave my heart to Him, and that's made all the difference."

Cami shifted uncomfortably. "Well, you are different. I got to hand you that." Her eyes searched the floor for an uncomfortable moment. Clearing her throat, she glanced up and pointed at the whiteboard. "Now, getting back to more pressing issues, from my vantage point in the lounge, I could observe the movements of nearly everyone on the main level. Carnes and the maid were right on the time but these others ... well. Their numbers just don't add up. They are covering for each other."

"And who was covering for you?"

Feigning offense, she said, "Why Trace, don't you trust me?"

I washed down the last bite of pizza with a swig and wiped my mouth. "Like President Reagan once said, 'Trust, but verify.'"

One of her shoulders lifted and fell gently back in place, "Okay, you got me there. But my alibi is solid. Go ask Evelyn or Donna. They'll tell you the same thing. I was in the Lounge until 11:00."

"With all that coffee in your system, you didn't have to take a break to, uh, powder your nose, so to say?"

A chagrined expression crept over Cami's face. "Oh yes, but I was gone for only a minute, maybe two."

"Enough time to run upstairs, shove Monica down and come back before you were missed?"

Cami slumped onto the only other seat in the living room. "Yeah, you got me dead to rights. Or was it enough time for me not to see who really did it. You ever thought about that, Mr. Smarty Pants?"

I picked up the stack of yellowed papers I'd gotten from Susan and placed them on the coffee table. Its nicks and scratches lent it a measure of character. For a moment, I considered telling her about what I learned from reading them but since she hadn't noticed what I'd done, I left them where they were. Being careful not to give Wag an excuse to take a bite out of me, I perched my hip on the arm of the couch and studied the timeline.

"Come to think of it, I looked at my watch at exactly 11:00 p.m. I distinctly remember hearing the clock downstairs gong out the time. But then, sometime later, it gonged again. That seemed funny since it wasn't eleven or twelve o'clock. I was so sleepy I hadn't given it much thought until just now."

"Which means?" Cami interjected.

"It means someone tampered with the clock and that everyone's times are off. How long were you gone on your potty break?"

Cami's forehead clouded. Her eyes searched the floor as if the answer lay somewhere at her feet. Her voice grew vague. "Oh, I don't know. It wasn't that long. When I came back, Luciano and Sanchez were still in the billiard room. That's when I heard the clock."

"Which time, the first time or the second?"

She offered me a quizzical expression.

"That's what I thought. What about Nate? Where was he?"

Cami thought for a minute. "Nate said he and the others were in the game room until 11:30, but again, the time was off. From what I gathered after you were arrested, the game ended around 10:45 in real time."

I rubbed the stubble on my chin, remembering I'd not shaved this morning. It was a routine I'd not gotten into yet ... I'd even considered growing a beard. "So what was he doing from then till he went to bed, eating cookies?" I picked up the red dry-erase marker and drew a big question mark over his name, then divided the white-board in half and wrote Motive.

"Okay, obviously someone killed Monica. What would be their motive?"

Cami grabbed the blue marker and wrote her name. "If I killed her, which I didn't, but if I did, it would have been because she stole my job."

I took the marker from her hand and wrote my name. "If I did it, which I didn't, but for the record, if I did, it would have been because she drove me to it. I'd claim insanity, if I had to do it all over."

Picking up on the theme, Cami took the red marker and wrote Nate Peterson's name. "Let's start with him. What does he have to gain by killing Monica?"

"Why not start with Luciano?"

"I guess you haven't heard."

"Heard what? I've been out of the loop you might say."

Cami gawked at me. "Don't they have television in prison?"

"Yeah, they have TV's, but all they'd let us watch were old reruns, SOAPs and game shows. Go ahead, ask me a trivia question."

"Trace."

"Okay, okay, I'm off topic, but I do know a lot of trivia."

"Trace. Luciano died several months ago."

Hands in surrender, I tried to refocus. "Okay, I didn't know, but with the old man dead, I'd have to put my money on Nate, too, but what about Antonio?"

"I, I don't think Antonio was in any condition to murder anyone."

"Oh? How so?" I asked.

Cami's shoulders stiffened. "Take my word for it. He was in no condition to do much."

I wanted to press the issue, but something in her tone told me to leave it alone. She'll fill in that blank when she's good and ready. Feeling overwhelmed, I slouched next to Wag and lifted the notes I'd made on a legal pad. "There were just too many possibilities. Nearly anyone could have pushed her down the stairs." In frustration, I tossed it aside.

"Not so fast. We both know the governor was best buds with old man Luciano. With him lining up his candidacy for the presidency, he couldn't afford for that information to get out. That's why he got out of there before the police arrived."

"You'd make a good detective. We'd make a great team if you ever want to quit your day job," I said with a smile.

A stray hair caught in the corner of her mouth and she brushed it back. "And remember what I told you the night of the murder. Monica told me how she squeezed the Chief of Staff position out of the gov."

I paused and looked over my shoulder. "How in Sam-hill did she do that?"

Cami shrank down next to me on the couch making Wag shift. "Earlier that evening, the booze had loosened her tongue a bit. She told me she'd connected the gov with Luciano, that he had paid her a million dollars to keep it quiet. Actually, on second thought, I think Monica knew something else."

"Why'd ya say that?"

Giving me a nervous shrug, she bit her lip. "I don't know. Call it a woman's intuition, call it a sixth sense, but there definitely was something going on between the two of them, and it had to do with that necklace she was wearing."

"That necklace," I said. "There is something about that necklace which makes me think I'm not seeing the bigger picture.

"Come to think of it Trace, I don't remember seeing it around Monica's neck when they carried her out to the coroner's car."

"Well, now we're getting somewhere. Why didn't you tell that in open court? You could have saved me six years in the penitentiary."

Her expression darkened, and I knew I'd hurt her feelings. She dropped her head. "Do you know what that would have done to my career, not to mention the governor's?"

I slipped from the couch and knelt in front of her. "Do you know what another second of the lethal concoction would have done to my career?"

A tear coursed down Cami's cheek. She brushed it aside, then buried her face in her hands and began to weep bitterly. "I know and it has haunted me ever since."

I wanted to take her in my arms and hold her but didn't know if I should. Shoving Wag aside, I retook my seat next to her and placed my arm over her heaving shoulders.

"Trace, I'm so sorry. I nearly got you executed. Can you forgive me?" Her sobs brought a lump to my throat and tears to my eyes. Swallowing hard, I leaned in close and brushed aside a few strands of hair from her face. Then, I took her by the hands and held them. Her icy fingers closed around mine and squeezed.

"Cami, because Jesus has forgiven me of far worse things, I forgive you."

And that was the simple truth.

It was like a weight had been lifted from her shoulders. She took a cleansing breath and let it out slowly. "Oh Trace." She buried her face in my chest and sobbed.

Not sure how to respond to such an outpouring of emotion, I just held her close and thanked the Lord for His grace. All at once, I became aware of Wag's large head resting on my lap. It occurred to me I had a friend for life.

After several minutes, Cami regained her composure and looked up. Her puffy red eyes, now streaked with mascara, spoke of pain, of guilt, and of love. She blinked away the last of her tears, and continued, "Getting back to what I was saying, Nate had a very good reason to bump off his wife."

I retook my position in front of the white-board. "And why's that?"

"Rumor had it that Monica was seeing someone. I can't prove it, but I wouldn't put it past her."

"Cami, having an affair wouldn't be motive enough to kill for … would it?"

"It depends. If word got out that Sanchez was having an affair with Nate Peterson's wife, the scandal would have blown his shot at the governor's seat. And, I might add, he would have lost any chance he had at getting the party's nomination for the presidency down the road."

"Sounds like a great motive for Sanchez to kill her." I drew a big red circle around Rafael Sanchez's name.

"Yes, but it could also have messed up any chance Nate might have had at getting his brother out of prison. He'd still be rotting in prison to this day."

"What was his brother in the slammer for?"

Cami's forehead creased as she tried to remember. "His brother was a doctor, charged with malpractice. Allegedly several women died on the operating table, and he was the attending physician. Others claimed he permanently mutilated them. I mean sterilized them, including Monica. She sued him for malpractice and received a sizable settlement. It got national coverage for weeks. Then, when Sanchez signed Nate's brother's release it all hit the fan. It nearly cost him his governor's seat."

"So bumping off Monica could have solved both Nate's and Rafael's problem." Picking up the marker, I drew a big red circle around Nate's name.

"You got that right, Trace."

"When did the governor sign the release papers?"

Her fingers came up one by one. "About three years ago."

"Does this doctor have a name?"

Cami bit the corner of her lip. "Yeah, Nelson Peterson."

The name meant nothing to me. "Where's he living now?"

She shook her head, "I don't know. For all we know, he could be back in business anywhere."

Chapter Twenty-Five

Nelson stood outside Lily's small bedroom.

She had been listless ever since she and her step-father had returned from her appointment with her therapist. The fact that Nate called her physician to make a house call worried him.

With his hand on the doorframe, he watched in silence as the doctor assessed Lily's condition.

After taking her temperature, the doctor straightened, the lines on his face were deep with concern. "She's burning up."

"I know, she's been that way all day," Nate added, peering through the blinds as if he expected someone.

"How long has she been sick?" the doctor asked, as he listened to her pulse.

Nate turned away from the window and paced across the floor, hands in his pockets. "She's been complaining about not feeling good for a while. I chalked it up to female stuff. But ever since her visit with her shrink, she's been sullen and uncommunicative. I think she's depressed."

The doctor stood.

"Depression doesn't cause a fever. She's got a bug or something. I'm going to prescribe Theraflu for her flu symptoms and Remeron to help with depression. Let's give it a few days and see if that helps."

Nate stopped his pacing and pulled his hand from his pocket. "You are aware that her twenty-first birthday is in less than two weeks, aren't you? I'm planning on a big celebration, and I don't want her doped up."

Returning his level gaze, the doctor nodded his head. "Here, get this filled as soon as possible." Tearing a sheet of paper from his script pad, he handed it to Nate. "If it's the flu, she'll be over it by then. If not, we'll know soon enough. As far as the depression is concerned, well, we'll just have to hope for the best."

He gave Nelson a slight nod and headed down the stairs.

$$\$ \$ \$$

Reaching into his pocket, Nate fingered a small bottle of pills he'd acquired on the black market.

The small yellow pill he'd ground to power and slipped into her milkshake had the same symptoms as the flu with the added benefit of causing its victim to go into a deep depression. He smiled at his creativity and followed the doctor down to the main floor. His work was almost complete. A few more doses and he would be a rich man.

Chapter Twenty-Six

My phone buzzed interrupting my concentration.

It was Monday afternoon and Cami left after our foray into Nate's garage. Not having someone to dog-sit, she elected to leave Wag with me rather than put him in a Doggy-Hotel.

I wasn't expecting a call from anyone. Since I'd not given my phone number out, and with Cami busy traveling with the governor, I was surprised to hear it ring. Chalking it up to a salesman, I nearly let it go to voice mail. However, since I'd not set it up yet, I punched the green button and waited for what I expected to be the usual, "don't hang up this is a very important call."

When the recording didn't start, I said, "Hello?"

"Is this Trace O'Reilly?" There was a slight tremble in the caller's voice and I couldn't tell if it was nerves or age.

The voice was unfamiliar. "Who is this?"

For a moment dead air filled the connection. When the caller finally spoke, it was in hushed tones.

"This is Carnes, the Butler. I am calling on behalf of Mr.—"

"—Yes, I remember you. How'd you get this number?"

"It doesn't matter," the butler shot back. "Now listen very closely. You may have heard the news about Rose Berettas' passing. Don't believe it. She is still with us, but not for long. You need to get up here, immediately. I don't think she'll make it through the night."

The line went dead before I could ask for details.

$$$

The forty-five minute drive from Sacramento along Highway 50 east to the Beretta estate brought back many memories, some good, some not so good.

I hoped this time would be more productive than the last.

As I approached the gate protecting the Beretta mansion, I rolled down the window and brought my vintage Renault to a halt. Elbow on the door frame, I glanced up at the guard.

"Hello, officer." I recognized the guard as the same one who pounded on my door the night I was arrested.

The years hadn't been too kind to the man. His stocky frame was stooped with age. The older man pushed back his uniform hat and peered down at me. "Well, if it isn't Mr. O'Reilly. I thought by now, you'd have learned to stay away from us law-abiding folk."

"Same old Larry … just as friendly as ever," ignoring the acidic welcome. "I'm here to see Rose Beretta."

The guard hiked up his britches, "She's in there, but not for much longer. Bring that junker inside, but park it on the grass. Mr. Beretta doesn't take too kindly to oil spots on his driveway."

I followed his instructions and parked it off to the side. With a gut-wrenching squeak, I forced the car door open, pulled myself out, and handed the rickety guard the keys.

Glancing at the rusty vehicle, I said, "Ain't she a beauty? Take good care of her and give her a wash while you're at it. Now I mustn't keep the lady waiting. Oh, and don't worry about the dog. His name is Wag and he's my security system." I turned and strode up the fern lined path I'd walked over six years ago.

After ringing the doorbell, I stepped back and listened. Leather heels on hardwood crescendoed until they stopped. A moment later, the door swung open and I was rewarded with Carnes' kind smile.

"Good day, sir. Thank you for coming so quickly. Please, Antonio is expecting you." The gentleman bowed slightly and ushered me in.

Things hadn't changed much since my last visit. The overstuffed couches, the fire in the fireplace beckoned me to sit and rest a while, but I had neither the time nor interest.

"Hello, Mr. O'Reilly." Antonio's voice echoed throughout the dimly lit parlor. He approached, hand extended. I accepted his proffered hand and shook it warmly. For a moment, we stood, considering each other. Antonio, though much younger than his father, bore many of his features. A pair of steely grey eyes peered at me from under a level brow. His firm jaw-line communicated decisiveness. His grip felt like an iron fist inside a velvet glove.

Antonio coughed slightly and stepped back. "I asked Carnes to call you, thanks for coming so quickly. Mother is slipping fast; would you please follow me." He turned and marched down the hall into the private residence side of the mansion. Pausing at a bedroom door, he laid his hand on the knob and glanced up. "You know my father passed a few months ago, didn't you?"

"Yes, sorry for your loss."

His countenance changed, and I couldn't tell if it was grief or relief. "Thank you, don't be long," he said and swung the door open.

Chapter Twenty-Seven

After taking a seat next to the dying woman's bed, I lifted Ms. Beretta's arthritic hand and waited. She opened her eyes and smiled. "I was wondering if you were going to stop by and thank me for saving your life." The oxygen tube beneath her nose moved as she spoke.

"Ms. Beretta, I'd heard you'd died."

She gave him a toothless grin. "It seems, 'news of my demise has been greatly exaggerated,' to quote an old friend of mine." The statement brought a deep chuckle, followed by a cough.

"Yes, Ms. Beretta, you're like the Energizer Bunny, you just keep going and going."

"I think by now you may call me Rose. Now, come closer." The woman's eyes burned with passion. The same passion I'd seen when she spoke about her husband.

I leaned close.

"I know why you're here." Her breath tickled my ear, but I resisted the urge to pull away for fear of missing a word.

"And why's that, Rose?"

"Information," she wheezed.

Out of the corner of my eye, I caught a glimpse of an impish twinkle in her eyes and knew. "I really appreciate what you did for me. I am in your debt."

She waved her hand, IV tubes and all. "It was the right thing to do. I couldn't have lived with myself if I let an innocent man die for nothing." Her words came in whispered tones. She held my gaze until I felt uncomfortable. "I know who killed that evil woman ... Monica Peterson." Her dark eyes simmered with hate. "It's just so confusing though. First I saw him in one place and then I saw him in another. But I know what I saw. He pushed her down the stairs."

The news nearly knocked me from my seat. My heart slammed against my ribs and I asked, "Who, Rose? Who killed Monica?"

Her head drooped. Her strength was failing, and I feared we would lose her before I got the answers I sought.

"I overheard two men talking about killing her. One of them threatened me ... made me swear to keep my mouth shut or he would destroy the Beretta family."

Her eyelids closed and I thought that was the end.

After a long, breathless pause, she inhaled.

So did I.

Her eyes flickered open. "I'm sorry it took so long." A tear coursed down her cheeks. "But some things were not in my control. I had to wait for the right time."

"I'm grateful you did. But Rose, if it was Luciano, he has already gone to his reward. He's past the judgment of men—"

"—it wasn't him, and I'm not saying that because he's my boy." She gasped for air and the doctor entered the room and adjusted her oxygen supply, then cleared his throat.

I knew my time was up.

So was Ms. Beretta's.

Her eyes fluttered and she gasped for air again. "Let me ask you a question."

Leaning closer I said, "Yes, anything."

"Anything? Would you do *anything* to save your family?"

Her question brought me upright. "I don't understand the question, Miss Rose."

"I think you do, but you haven't got the answer … yet. By the way, have you found the necklace?"

I wasn't sure if she was lucid or not as nothing had been mentioned about any necklace prior to that moment. What connection was there between saving my family and some necklace? "Necklace? What necklace?"

Her chest rose and fell as she struggled to breathe. "Young man, if you find the necklace, you will find Monica's killer. If you don't know about it by now, then forget I ever mentioned it. There are some thing's best not known." The fire in her eyes faded.

I knew I wasn't going to get anymore from my friend. Straightening my legs, I stood, leaned over and placed a kiss on her wrinkled brow. "Good-bye Rose. I will always cherish our conversation by the fireplace."

She gave my hand a final squeeze and relaxed. For the second time in as many days, tears scalded my cheeks. The doctor entered and began fidgeting with the tubes.

I knew it was time to leave so I stepped from her room more determined to find the answers I sought.

Antonio met me outside her room. "Thank you for seeing her," he repeated. Like his father, he was the perfect gentlemen. "Did she say anything, I mean, anything of importance?" The question struck me as odd.

"No, we didn't have that long and I think she was a bit disoriented." I paused, not sure whether or not I should mention the necklace. I decided to keep it to myself. "She was a good woman."

He nodded sullenly and we parted company.

However, as I retraced my steps, I couldn't help but feel his piercing eyes following me.

As I crossed in front of the stairs, my breathing shallowed and I was overwhelmed with the sense of falling. What must it have been like to have fallen backward down these very steps? I wondered. I stopped at the landing and peered up at the grandfather clock. Its faithful ticking beat out a steady rhythm.

Movement caught my attention as Carnes signaled for me to step into an alcove.

"Sir, I must apologize for my memory lapse, but there is something I think you should know." His voice came low, raspy.

I held his gaze, giving the man time to gather his thoughts. "Yes, Carnes, what is it?" I prompted.

The elderly man, now in his eighties, appeared gaunt, more bone-weary than the last time I'd seen him. "Well, it seemed a small thing back then and still, it may be nothing, but—" he paused and let his eyes wander around the room.

I waited patiently. "Go on."

The older gentleman cleared his throat. "It was the night we celebrated Mr. Sanchez's and your birthdays."

"You mean, the night Monica was murdered … the night I was arrested for committing it?"

Carnes shifted uncomfortably. "Yes, that's the night. Luciano had me hire a new caterer to serve. Our regular caterer was booked that night. We had to rush around to find a reputable company who could pass Luciano's scrutiny. For the most part, they seemed competent, but there was one man who appeared a bit clumsy. There was just something odd about him, like it as his first day on the job."

For a moment, I stared at the man. So this was the big secret he'd been holding for all these years? Nodding politely, I backed away.

"Well, thank you, Carnes, I'll put it in my notes and check it out. Could you provide me with the name of the caterer?"

Carnes produced a crisp, clean calling card with the catering company's name and phone number on it. It was obvious he'd kept it safe all these years. I hoped it held as much promise for me as it did Carnes. Pocketing the card, I turned and continued my trek. As I reached the door, I paused. Carnes had shadowed me and extended his hand to open the door.

"By the way, did you happen to notice whether or not, Monica was wearing the necklace when you found her?

Carnes stiffened, the muscles in his jaw tightened. "I'm afraid I can't say."

"Can't or won't?" I hated being so rough on the old man, but I had to know.

"There is one other thing—"

His eyes shifted in the direction of Miss Rose's room as his pager vibrated.

"You were saying?"

"I'm sorry. I must go. Please excuse me." He turned abruptly and headed to the back of the residence leaving me with more questions than answers. Why did he avoid answering me? And what was he going to tell me before his pager went off? I made a mental note of it and returned to my car.

Chapter Twenty-Eight

With my windows down, I sped along the highway, a light trail of gray smoke fouled the fresh mountain air behind me.

To my left was the lush prairie of the Sacramento Valley. To my right, the hill country of El Dorado, Folsom, and Rancho Cordova. It was a beautiful drive, one I wished I could share with Cami. But today I had more pressing business, so I sat back and enjoyed the drive. Wag enjoyed it too, as he hung his head out the window and lapped up the cool breeze ruffling his hair and causing his ears to flap. It was against my better judgment to dog-sit, but to appease Cami, I conceded. With her schedule, she didn't need a dog, and it was becoming obvious I was the de facto owner of the beast. My cell phone chirped, interrupting my thoughts.

"Hello?"

"Trace." The tension in her voice cut through static and wind noise.

"Cami, let me pull over. I can barely hear you." A moment later, I found a wide place on the shoulder of the winding road overlooking the prairie. The view was spectacular. Too bad I'm alone, I thought.

The car rolled to a gentle stop, and I picked up the phone. "What's up?"

"Trace, I was talking with a few attorneys and one of them just so happened to be the executor of the Peterson estate."

"Estate? I didn't know Monica had an estate."

"Yep, she does. You know that big settlement I told you about? Well it's real, that along with a million dollars. And it's been sitting in a bank earning interest for the last six-plus years."

I rubbed the back of my neck. It stung and I realized the sun had gotten to it. The stress of the case was playing havoc with my nerves. I looked forward to the time when this mess would be over.

"So how does that play into the plot?" no sooner had I asked the question than I knew the answer.

"Motive!"

"Motive? We already established the motive. It's either revenge, jealousy, anger, or to silence her. Only you knew about the money. Maybe you murdered her after all," he said half kiddingly.

"Trace ..." the pain in her voice came through loud and clear in that one word. "How dare you accuse me, you had every reason to kill her as much I did. She hated you, and you hated her." Her words came in clipped phrases.

I knew I'd hurt her, but I had to say it. In my mind, Cami's own words rang— "Trust no one."

"I'm sorry, I'm sorry. I didn't mean to hurt your feelings. This case is driving me nuts."

The silence on the other end was excruciating.

Finally, Cami spoke, "You're forgiven, but don't doubt me again, and especially," she took a halting breath, "don't accuse me."

I felt duly reprimanded. "You're right, I shouldn't have said that. Can you meet me at my place?"

"No, the governor's got me running all over the state. I won't be home until tomorrow. Oh, and by the way, what I really called about is this, that attorney told me he'd been contacted by—" a wash of static garbled her next words. "—to execute the Will the day before Lily's twenty-first birthday. That's next week. Doesn't that seem odd?"

My blood pressure spiked and I could feel my pulse throbbing in my ears. "Cami, who did you say arranged the reading of the Will?"

A dull hiss filled the connection and I bit back the urge to lash out. It was my own fault for choosing a cheap wireless company. Frustrated, I tossed the phone on the seat next to Wag causing him to growl. "Sorry, buddy. If you're going to be my partner, you're going to have to get used to my outbursts."

By now, I had lost all interest in the scenic beauty of the landscape. My mind focused on stopping the execution of the Will.

Chapter Twenty-Nine

T he whiteboard located in the middle of my small two-bedroom apartment stared mockingly back at me as I sought for answers.

On one side of the room was the threadbare couch. Its rumpled cushions having seen too many bottoms now supported my only companion … Wag.

My call to the catering service proved to be a dead-end. Not that I'd hadn't expected it. Like with most of my efforts, it was a waste of time. By now, most of the employees had moved on. As I thanked the last person I'd been transferred to, my luck changed.

The man's New England accent stood in sharp contrast to the laid back vernacular of most Californians.

"So who wants to know?" he asked.

I knew with my notoriety, telling him I was the guy accused of killing the DA's wife would get me nowhere. So I took on my role-playing routine. "I am an insurance adjuster with Phelps, Whitney and Barnes, and I just left Antonio Beretta's residence. It seems Rose Beretta has died and the Butler, Mr. Carnes, gave me your calling card and asked me to call."

The New Englander's tone softened. "Antonio? Don't know him. But Luciano … now there is a stand-up guy.

He used my services many times. How can I be of service to you?"

This was it. No more smoke and mirrors. I had to ask. "Yes, well, the last time your company served at the mansion, they found some very expensive jewelry missing. A necklace, to be exact and there is a sizable finder's fee being offered to the one who recovers it."

The New Englander expressed his thoughts in a most inappropriate way. "That was what … over six years ago. How am I supposed to remember who I hired and who worked for me that long ago?"

"Yes, I can understand your shock," I said, trying to calm the man down. "Your employees were completely vetted. You must have a record of them. Could you check?"

I heard more cursing and shuffling of papers. Finally, the man returned. "That night, we had a last minute substitute. One of my servers just didn't show up for work. I'm not sure who authorized it, but there was a new hire placed on the roster."

Hope rose. "Do you have a name?"

"No, I'm sorry. Now what did you say your name was Mr.—?"

My heart tripped. I was so close. Quickly, I hung up before I got myself into trouble.

"So Carnes was right. There was someone who didn't belong in the mansion. I wonder why I hadn't noticed him. All at once, the image of a servant picking up my coat and offering to take it to the cloak closet came to mind. I wonder if that was him. He did act a little strange.

I need to ask Cami if she noticed him lurking around. Maybe he's our mystery man."

Closing my eyes, I tried to think back to that night. I had taken my overcoat off and was wearing only my sports coat. Funny thing about that … there were no buttons missing from my coat. I knew that because after I was released from prison, I checked. They were all there. So whose button was in Monica's hand? The only other person wearing a sports coat was Sanchez. But getting a look at it was impossible. And then there was the two men arguing in the solarium … the man and two women arguing in the upstairs landing, the mysterious man. Who were they?"

As I considered the many possibilities, I felt the weight of Wag's head on my leg. His eyes twitched back and forth.

"I bet you want to go for a walk."

Wag sprang up and danced in a circle. I pushed myself up and collected his leash. After tethering the two of us together, I opened the door and followed him out. The walk did us both a lot of good. He sought the first shrub he could find while a dozen scenarios fluttered around in my head like moths to a streetlight.

$$$

By the time we returned, I knew it was too late to do much.

"We'll just have to wait until morning, ol' buddy." Wag cocked his head in mock understanding.

Retaking my place in front of the white-board, I continued my inquiry. "Who would benefit the most from Lily's death?"

Wag yawned and acted interested. I picked up a red marker and drew a line across it and wrote, "Motives for killing Lily."

By now, I had a pretty good grasp of the situation. In a week, Lily would either be rich or dead. Time was running out.

"Okay. First, we can cross off Luciano. He died ten months ago. Next, is Sanchez. A million dollars could help his campaign, and since it was his money in the first place, it would make sense he would want to get it back. But it sure would complicate things." I put an X next to his name.

"Okay, who is next? Scanning the names, I put a large X next to Cami's name. Wag stood and pranced in a circle. "I take it you agree." Wag shook his head.

"Well, that leaves Nate. He had to have known about the money. He's been biding his time waiting until Lily turned twenty-one. Who knows what he plans to do with her then. He had to have killed Monica and for a multitude of reasons; jealousy, revenge, his reputation, screwing up his brother's release, and then there was the money. As Lily's guardian, he is the default recipient of the million. Should she die before her twenty-first birthday, all that money goes to him. Plus, if Lily really does know who killed her mother, the secret would die with her."

And all this, he's been blaming me, and he almost got away with it. In my professional opinion, he is suspect *numero uno*." Wag's two paws landed on my chest, nearly knocking me over. "Oh, so who's the lead inspector in this case now?"

Wag barked crisply.

"We need to take another peek at those files and check Nate's alibi against the new timeline."

As I paced across the tight space in my living room, my cell phone buzzed. Looking at the caller ID, I knew who it was.

"Yes Cami, Wag is just fine."

A chuckle echoed through the connection. "That's not why I called, but it's good to know."

"Well I'm glad you did. We got cut off as I was coming through the mountains and I didn't understand what you said about the Will."

She shifted the phone from one ear to the other. "I'm driving, so I can't go into much detail. But first, let me say, since you're her real dad, couldn't you appeal to the Family Court for guardianship?"

I stopped pacing. My heart pounded in my ears. Yes, she is my daughter, but since my divorce, I'd not been much of a father to her. I was either too busy building a career or too drunk because of it. Complicating the matter even further was the court-ordered mandate. With Lily turning twenty-one, that option seemed out of the question. And after my last encounter with her, I wasn't so sure she'd ever speak to me.

Cami's voice cut through the clutter and I heard her saying something about taking responsibility for my actions. I staggered to the couch and flopped on it.

"Cami, I don't know if that's such a good idea. These things take time and frankly, I'm not so sure she'll go along with the idea. The last time we spoke, she came close to cussing me out. And I know for sure, if Nate has anything to say in the matter, he will fight it all the way to the Supreme Court."

"Trace, get a spine."

A thick veil of silence hung between the two phones. Finally, she spoke, this time a determined edge to her voice. "Look, Trace, talk with her family doctor."

"Her family doctor? I can't just go to his office and pump him for information. There are HIPPAA laws and privacy concerns. He'll never talk to me in a million years."

"Trace, you're not listening. My uncle thinks there is something fishy going on. One call, that's all I'm asking. Here's his number."

I jotted it down only to get her off my back, but she wasn't so easily pacified. "Are you going to make the call?"

Feeling boxed in, I conceded. "Cami, if I ever need an assistant, you've got the job."

"Fat chance of that. Call me as soon as you get off the phone with the doc."

$$$

Twenty minutes later, I hung up from the doctor and hit the redial.

"What did he say?" Cami asked.

"What you probably already knew, that Lily is sick. He told me, off the record of course, that her symptoms were, 'inconsistent with his analysis.'"

"Meaning?"

"Meaning, someone may be poisoning or drugging her."

"Trace, I'm not telling you how to run your family, but if I were you, I'd get down to the Family Court and demand immediate custody. But first, let me make a phone call and grease the wheels. You know that lawyer friend I mentioned?"

"Yes, why?"

"He's my uncle and he owes me big time for all the business I shoveled his direction. Let me see what he can do. Maybe all you'll need to do is sign a few papers. He'll do the rest. Within twenty-four hours, you'll get your daughter back."

My heart did a back-flip. I loved Lily, though she probably didn't love me. Yet in my heart, I knew she would eventually come around. But that was the problem … I didn't have twenty-four hours.

For the second time in as many days, I was torn between saving Lily and catching a murderer. This time the choice was clear. Grabbing the leash, I clipped Wag's collar to it, shrugged on my overcoat and dashed to my car.

"Come on Wag, let's save Lily."

Chapter Thirty

It was nearly 4:45 p.m. when my car rumbled to a stop in front of the Sacramento Court House.

Amidst a billow of exhaust, I got out, checked my watch. I had very little time to spare and no time to waste.

"Stay," I ordered. Wag ogled me with pleading eyes. "Don't look at me that way. You know they wouldn't let you in so don't ask."

Wag whined and assumed a resting position.

"I can't believe I'm talking to a dog," I muttered as I dashed up the steps.

An elderly guard was about to lock the doors when I squeezed through the narrow opening.

"Hey mister, you can't come in here. We're about to close up'" He was clearly bothered.

"Which way to the Family Court?" I asked between gulps of air.

The older man pointed with his nose to the elevator. "Third floor, but you'd better hurry."

A clerk had just exited an elevator on her way out. I broke into a run and reached it before the doors closed. Sending up a quick prayer, I pushed the button. The doors slid closed, and I counted the seconds until it delivered me to the third level.

Barely squeezing through the receding doors, I made a bee-line for the Family Court. I swung the door open and found the courtroom empty. The bailiff was just locking up.

"Is, the judge here?" I asked, panting.

The bailiff, not accustomed to having his routine altered, glanced up. Frustrated, he said, "Are you Trace O'Reilly?"

"Yes, I am."

"The judge was expecting you, but I think you may have missed him."

"Can you check?"

The man nodded and disappeared behind a panel. A moment later, a hand appeared and waved me in.

Swallowing hard, I stepped through the paneled door and found the judge preparing to head out for a round of golf.

"Sir, I'm here on behalf of my daughter, Lily Peterson."

The judge eyed me warily, "And you are?"

"I'm Trace O'Reilly, her father."

The judge nodded. "Oh yes, I was expecting you a few hours ago. You just about missed me. Some hot-shot attorney called my office earlier and said he had all the papers in order, all you needed to do was to sign them. You know this is highly unusual. Normally these things take months."

"Months!" I blurted. "She doesn't have months."

The judge sat up straight, "What do you mean by that?" his voice grew tense.

"You see, sir, Lily is about to turn twenty-one. As a matter of fact, her birthday is tomorrow. When she does, she'll inherit a large sum of money."

A smile stretched across the judge's face. "Well then, congratulations to her."

"No, you don't understand. It's not that simple. If she doesn't reach her twenty-first birthday, the money goes to her next of kin who, in this case, is her step-father. I have it on good authority that she is sick, and is possibly being poisoned."

The judge's hand shot up. "That's a serious charge. Who told you this?"

"Her doctor."

"And you believe him?"

"I have no reason not to."

"Can he prove his suspicions?"

"I suppose so. He examined her less than a week ago and told me he was very concerned for her safety."

The judge snatched up the phone and dialed 9-1-1. "Mr. O'Reilly, you don't need custody. You need the police. I'll call them and have a unit arrive within the hour."

The judge scribbled his name on the documents and pushed them across his desk. "Sign on the marked spaces. I'll have them notarized by the end of the day. Now hurry."

The air in my lungs grew cold as I followed the judge's instructions. I was never so glad to sign so many pages in my life if it meant saving Lily. When I finished, I thanked the judge and dashed from his chambers. I had to get to Nate's house.

As the elevator descended, I speed-dialed Cami. "Cami, it worked," I said between gulps of air. "I signed the papers and the judge had them notarized. He is sending a squad car to the Peterson's residence as we speak but I want to get there first. Can you drop what you're doing and meet me there?

"Yeah sure, I'll come as fast as possible," she said. The tension in her voice was palpable.

In thirty minutes, I skidded to a stop in front of Nate Peterson's house. A moment later, Cami arrived.

"The police aren't here yet, but we don't have time to wait. Let's go." Grabbing the leash, I led Wag to the front door.

Finding it locked, I lifted my foot and kicked. The door jerked open and I bounded in followed by Wag.

I quickly assessed the living room. "This place is a mess. There must have been a brawl in here." An overturned couch and broken lamps littered the floor.

Cami took a sharp breath and ran for the stairs. "I'll check on Lily," she said taking two at a time with Wag close at her heels.

After inspecting the other rooms located on the first floor, I headed for the garage. One of Nate's cars was missing. I made a mental note of it and headed to Nate's loft office. One look and I realized we were too late. The drawers to the filing cabinets hung open, their contents gone. Clenching my fists, I cursed under my breath.

Movement behind me stole my breath. I whirled around ready to strike whoever it was. Cami stood in the doorway. Her face was flushed, her eyes wild.

"She's missing, Lily's gone!"

Feeling the air escape my lungs, I slumped into an old recliner. "So are the files. Whoever took Lily, must have taken them too."

Wag, who had been sniffing around the area, barked sharply. "Quiet Wag, we're trying to think."

He ignored her pleas and began scratching on an unopened box.

"I wonder what's gotten into him. He's never acted like that," she said, eyeing the cardboard box.

Curious, I stood and began inspecting its contents. Letting out a low whistle, I said, "Cami, would you get a look at this?" handing her the paper.

Cami froze as she held the papers. "Lily remembers all right. Her memory is back, and her life is hanging by a thread."

Reaching into the box, she picked up several more pictures, "Look Trace, these are exactly the same, and there are dozens of them."

She was so close, her breath rustled along my neck telegraphing my brain to go into overdrive. With my pulse at a hundred twenty beats a minute, I willed myself to breathe, to think, to concentrate. "Lily had been trying to tell what she saw for years, and Nate knew it. He must have been the one who took her and the files."

"Yes, but Trace, there are two people in the picture, not one. Who do you suppose the other person is?"

I pulled from her personal space and tried to focus. This wasn't happening, Cami's closeness, Lily's memory, the pictures, the Will, the money, her birthday. My brain slammed into high gear. With renewed focus, I began rummaging through another box. Triumphantly, I lifted a photograph. "Him!" I said, pointing at the picture.

Cami's face blanched. "That's Nate."

"No it's not … it's his twin … it's Nelson."

Dashing back down the steps, I rounded the corner and nearly stumbled over a medical bag. "This isn't good," I muttered.

A moment later, Wag let out a sharp yip.

"What is it Wag?" Cami's question morphed into a scream as she walked around the only other car in the garage.

My blood curdled. In an instant, I was at her side as her knees buckled. Lowering her to the concrete, I followed her shocked gaze.

The body of one of the Peterson's lay inches away from her, his face bludgeoned beyond recognition. Instinctively, I placed my two fingers on the side of the man's neck. There was no pulse.

"He's dead, Peterson is dead," I heard myself repeating. "I don't understand. Why would anyone want to kill him? Say what you want about Nate, he didn't deserve this."

Cami pushed herself up on wobbly legs and leaned heavily against the car, hand on her forehead. "You gotta get out of here. Your fingerprints are all over the place. If they didn't get you for murdering Monica, they certainly will for murdering her husband."

I stepped to a cluttered workbench, snatched a pair of pliers, and picked up the tire tool. I recognized immediately as coming from my car. How it got there, I could only guess, but it probably happened when I came here the first time. What a jerk, I chided myself. You walked right into this one.

"This is a setup if ever there was one." I jammed the tire tool between my belt and slacks. "If we're going to save Lily, we'd better hurry. Whoever grabbed her has at least an hour lead on us." I took a step toward my car.

"Wait a minute. We can't just leave the scene of a crime. You know that."

I paused mid-stride. "Right now, police don't think too kindly of me. With my fingerprints everywhere and the judge knowing I was headed here, it stands to reason the police will think I had an altercation with him and killed him. I'll be back in the slammer in the blink of an eye."

The shrill warble of a police car echoed off the surrounding buildings, and I knew I was out of time.

"Okay," Cami said, "You go to your apartment. After I get done here, I'll catch up."

"What will you tell the police if they ask about me?" I asked, looking over my shoulder as the sirens grew louder.

Cami took one last look at the body and shuddered, then returned her attention to me. "I'll do my best to sanitize the area."

"You can't do that. You might destroy important evidence. There's a real killer out there and the police need to get him. You'll just have to come up with a good excuse, or I'm dead meat."

Hand to her throat, she nodded resolvedly. "Okay, I'll think of something, now go."

I sprinted to my car with Wag close behind. "Wag, you stay with Cami. I'll see you in a little while." I must be going crazy ... talking to dogs, I thought.

As I rounded the corner, I caught a glimpse of a police cruiser as it pulled to a stop in the driveway.

Chapter Thirty-One

A fter satisfying the police's questions, Cami left the Peterson's residence.

Hoping to find Trace at his apartment waiting for her, she was disappointed to find the place empty. It had been nearly four hours since Trace had disappeared and Cami was getting worried. Had he launched out on his own in search of Lily's abductor? Where would he even begin to search? And who was that mystery man Trace pointed to in the picture? He looked like Nate, but it was impossible to know, not until the body in the morgue was identified

She guessed the connection only too late. Ten years after Trace and Monica broke up, Monica married Nate Peterson. It was through Nate's efforts that Nelson was released from prison. Apparently, he had moved in with his brother after his release. One of the two men killed the other. Only after an autopsy would they know who it is. In the meantime, the other man had Lily. His motives clearly in question, but no doubt her money was at the root of it. Either way, Lily was in grave danger.

She had to reach Trace. Just the mention of his name brought back mixed emotions. Oh yes, she still had feelings for him ... deep feelings. When they'd first met, she fell in love with him almost immediately. But it wasn't long before she discovered that his real passion was booze and work and that she was just his mistress. Their brief encounter the night of Monica's death only accentuated the emptiness in her heart. Now that he was back in her life those old feelings began to stir. Wherever Trace was, she wanted to be with him, to support him, to encourage him, to stand by his side.

Her phone buzzed, making her jump.

Wag sprang to his feet at her sudden outburst. "Sorry Wag. I didn't mean to startle you."

$$$

"Help!"

My muffled cry brought a bevy of questions which I couldn't answer.

The gag my captors had stuffed in my mouth tasted like gasoline making it hard to breath, let alone keep my stomach in check. After four agonizing hours of being in that condition, my mouth felt like an overstuffed laundry bag.

To make matters worse, the knot on the back of my head throbbed with relentless ferocity. In the fading light, I knew I was in some type of warehouse, but I had no clue where.

Having left my cell phone in the car when I was roughed up by those thugs was a blessing and a curse. If I still had it on me, they surely would have destroyed it, but not being able to call anyone for help left me wondering how I'd ever be found.

$$$

"Trace, where are you?"

Cami hollered as the voice recorder clicked on for the fifth time. "Trace, call me as soon as you get this message," she repeated and ended the call. It was useless. Why would Trace call and not tell her where he was? Maybe it was one of those fanny-calls, the kind that happens when you sit on your phone wrong. That's what he gets for carrying the dumb thing in his back pocket. She tossed it on the couch.

The GPS.

She chided herself for not thinking of it earlier. Remembering the smartphone had a GPS tracking app, she crossed her fingers and touched the icon. Instantly a red blip appeared on her phone. It indicated the location of the phone somewhere in the Sacramento warehouse district along the railroad tracks.

Why would he be there? Maybe he got a lead and followed Lily's kidnapper there. Maybe he called for help because he was outnumbered. She didn't remember him applying for a firearm and even if he did, she doubted he had time to get one.

"C'mon, Wag, let's find Trace." Grabbing her phone and handbag, she dashed to her car with Wag leading the way.

The clock on her dashboard glowed 10 p.m. by the time she found Trace's car sitting not far from a decrepit warehouse. It looked like an accordion. Both its front and rear fenders were crumpled, but it looked drivable. *I wonder how that happened and why it's here. And where is Trace?* As she approached the building, her headlights flashed across the rusting door with the ominous warning to, "Keep Out!" Her heart dipped at the thought that Trace might be in there.

She slammed the car into park and shut off her engine. The night closed in around her. An eerie silence filled the stagnant air and she wished she had a gun. Being careful not to give away her position, she and Wag slipped quietly from her car and tiptoed to the building. Cell phone in one hand, Wag's leash in the other, she inched closer to the door. Like a bloodhound, Wag sniffed the concrete for any scent left by Trace. All at once, he became agitated and started scratching on the door.

A set of muddy tire tracks leading to and from the platform told her someone had recently been there. She just hoped whoever it was wouldn't come back. Peering through a grungy window, she saw nothing; no movement, no cars, no Trace.

Biting her lower lip, she pushed aside her fear and tugged on the door handle. It yielded, but not without its ball-bearings squealing angrily. In the distance, a dog barked, threatening to wake the dead. Wag growled but kept his vigil.

Inside, moonlight trickled through rusted cracks in the roof sending thin shafts of pale light to the floor. She flicked on her flashlight app and scanned the area. It was empty. As she crept deeper, long claw-like shadows dangled from the cables. Loose insulation moved with an inane rhythm as the wind blew through the cavernous building. With each step, the building seemed to groan under its own weight, and she wondered if it might come crashing down upon her at any moment. The further she pressed into the darkness, the less hopeful she became, yet her phone blinked out the signal. At least his phone is here, she thought.

From a black corner, a groan emerged. Chicken-skin crawled over her like ants. Hands slicking, she tried to moisten her dried lips. She tightened her grip on Wag's leash as he snarled and tugged her forward. Fighting the urge to run, Cami scanned the area until a set of greenish eyes glowed back at her.

"Trace?" In an instant, she was at his side.

He lay; face down, hands tied, mouth gagged and his phone next to him. It was a mystery how he'd managed to get it out of his pocket and make a call. But she was glad he did. The details could wait for another time. For now, all she wanted to do was hold him.

Taking care not to injure him any more than he was, she removed the gag and rolled him over. Sitting him upright, she tapped his cheek lightly.

"Trace, what happened to you?"

His eyes fluttered open and he groaned. "Cami, you came. I thought—"

"Shhhh, let me get you untied," she said. "Then we can talk."

After a moment, his mind seemed to clear. His eyes focused and he looked at Cami. "I was on my way home when a car came up behind me. It rammed into me causing me to lose control. My car hit the vehicle in front of me. The next thing I know, four guys jumped out and dragged me from my car. They tied and gagged me, then threw me into the lead car and brought me here."

"Why? Who were they and what did they want?"

He tried to piece things together but it seemed his mind refused to click into gear. "Remember the last case I broke before I was arrested?"

Her forehead wrinkling, Cami thought a moment. "No, why?"

"Well, I do, it was a gang of drug-dealers. I suspect they were working for the Beretta crime family though I can't prove it."

"Okay, so what's that got to do with this?"

He gritted his teeth as he pushed himself up from the oily floor. His shirt hung in loose array from someone ripping it open. It was stained with blood from the beating he'd received at the hands of the thugs. His lip was cut and his eye was nearly swollen shut, mute testimonies to the punishment he'd endured.

"I recognized one of the men who beat me up. Back then, he was just a low-level cash runner. But he grew up. Man did he pack a punch. Anyway, they wanted to know where the necklace was. I told them I didn't know anything about the necklace but they kept beating me anyway.

"The only person, outside of a very small circle who might have an interest in that necklace, could be Antonio Beretta. He quizzed me after I met with Rose. I don't think he believed me when I told him Rose passed away before divulging anything significant."

"Oh Trace, I'm so sorry." She pulled him close and felt the warmth of his body radiating through her sweater.

For a moment, all the years faded and it was like old times. She inhaled and let it out slowly. Leaning down, she pressed her lips against his.

Immediately, his arms wrapped around her, enfolding her in a tight embrace. Were it not for their current situation, she would have been satisfied to stay where they were. But there was a deranged man out there somewhere and he had Lily.

Chapter Thirty-Two

The metal exterior door squeaked interrupting the moment, sending my heart into overdrive.

Wag strained at his leash and let out a low growl.

"Stay Wag, we don't know who it is," I cautioned as leather heeled shoes scuffed the concrete.

Forcing my legs under me, I stood with Cami's help. A sharp snap echoed in the darkness followed by a beam of light. Its yellow shaft cut left and right like a lightsaber as it searched the shadowed corners, followed by heavy footsteps.

Fearing the thugs had returned to finish me off, I pushed Cami behind me and shielded her with my body. She wrapped her icy hands around my arm and clung to it. A moment later, the light beam swept across us and stopped.

"Mr. O'Reilly!? What are you doing here?" The voice was unfamiliar.

"Yeah, it's me. Who are you?" Holding my hands against the glare.

The beam lowered, and I heard the safety of a gun click. I wasn't sure if it was being flicked on or off, so I shoved Cami further back. My action caused Wag to offer the intruder a low growl.

"I'm Detective Troy Ashcroft," he said, holstering his weapon. I thought that was your car a few blocks from here. Who else would be driving around in that piece of junk?"

"Hey, it's not a piece of junk ... it's a classic antique," I fired back without thinking.

"Whatever," he shrugged. "I saw you driving it the other day when you came to the precinct."

"Oh, so you were one of the wise guys who thought I should have been executed."

The detective pulled his badge from his pocket and held it up.

"Are you here to hassle me, or help me, Detective Ashcroft?" I asked, squinting in the muted light.

"I'm here to help you. When I didn't see you in your classic antique," his fingers made air quotes, "I got suspicious and drove around the area looking for you. Then when she arrived," eyeing Cami as he spoke. "You are?"

Cami stepped out from behind me. Flipping her hair back, she stiffened and looked into the light. "Miss Stetson, Cami Stetson, I'm the governor's press secretary." She quipped.

A moment of recognition flashed across his eyes, and he relaxed his stance. "Oh yes, I know you. Well anyway, when Miss Stetson pulled up and began nosing around, I thought I'd come in and see what was going on. What happened? And don't tell me she did this to you." A half-smile hiked up the corner of his mouth.

I glanced at my shirt. "Yeah, I'm okay, and no, she didn't do this. Some old buddies caught me between cars, beat me up, and I ended up here. What's it to you?"

Troy pocketed his badge. "Hey, don't get testy with me, I'm the new guy. I saw how they treated you down at the police precinct. Frankly, I never believed those charges they slapped you with." He paused and glanced around.

"So tell me again why you are here?" he asked. Pulling a pen from a pocket guard and clicking it twice, he prepared to take notes.

Wag growled, and Cami tugged him closer.

"Like I said, some of the guys from a former gang I put behind bars, wanted to give me a welcome home party, that's all."

Satisfied, Ashcroft double clicked his pen and replaced it. "Got a name?"

"No,"

"A description?"

"It was too dark."

"You want to fill out a report?"

"No, and I don't need an ambulance."

Frustrated, Ashcroft softened his stance.

"But thanks. At least not all the guys on the force are against me. How about helping me to the car, we're in a bit of a hurry."

Twin furrows formed about Ashcroft's eyes. "Oh, I get it. All right, mums the word."

"No, it's not like you think. Miss Stetson needs to catch up with her boss."

Lifting his flashlight, Ashcroft scanned her again. "Okay, I get it. We can talk about a report later." He was not giving up so easily. I liked that about him. He took a step and stopped. Leaning over, he picked up an envelope. "Is this yours?"

I froze, not wanting to act too interested. "Uh, yes. I guess it must have fallen from my pocket." I reached out and grabbed it.

For a moment, he held it, not letting it go.

"Is there a problem, Ashcroft?"

He shook his head. "No, it's just a little unusual that your alleged attackers overlooked this."

"Alleged? I guess my injuries are alleged too."

Ashcroft released a nervous laugh. Giving Cami a quick glance, he said. "How did you know where to find Mr. O'Reilly?"

"GPS, my phone has a GPS app on it." His eyebrows hiked up.

"The department doesn't issue us grunts those fancy iPhones. I sure would like to have one." Eyeing the phone in her hand, he asked, "Mind if I take a look at it?"

I eyed him suspiciously. This guy is smooth. Comes across as a newbie, but he doesn't have me fooled for a minute. He's a pro if I'd ever seen one. I observed.

Giving Cami a nod, I took the phone and handed it to him. Cami eyed him carefully and from her body language, I knew she didn't like him.

He took a few minutes checking the settings, then handed it back. "Nice phone, I gotta get me one." He offered her a disarming smile, then turned to me.

"Your car's pretty beat up. Maybe I should give you a ride home. Wouldn't want anything to happen to you, now would we?"

I had no desire to ride in a police car.

Never, never, never.

But how my car got here was still a bit fuzzy. "I think she'll run, but thanks for the offer."

Ashcroft shook his head. "Okay, suit yourself."

As his footsteps faded, I leaned on Cami's arm and walked to the front of the building. "That stunt with your phone, I'll bet you dollars to donuts, he just farmed your call history."

"Yeah, and I'm guessing he's taking fingerprints and hair samples from your car as we speak."

"Smart guy," I whispered, "might be good to keep him close."

Cami leaned in. "Yeah, keep your friends close and your enemies closer. I don't like him."

I rubbed the knot on my head and winced. "At least I have someone in the department I can lean on for information. By the way, is Friday night open?"

She chuckled dismissively.

Chapter Thirty-Three

My muscles ached as I leaned on Cami's shoulder.

After a painful wait, I heard my car rumble to a start. A set of headlights blinked on and Detective Ashcroft pulled up in my Renault and stopped.

"That's some kind of classic car, Mr. O'Reilly. With a little work, you might get it looking like a real showpiece. Who knows, you could take it around to all the antique car shows … maybe win a prize."

I wasn't sure if he was kidding or not, so I let the comment pass. "Thanks, buddy, I owe you one. I believe we can make it from here."

Ashcroft nodded. "Okay Mr. O. You take care of yourself. How about I call you tomorrow?"

Grimacing at being called Mr. O, I dreaded the idea of having to answer any more questions. I took his proffered hand, and said, "Don't expect much help from me."

He nodded slowly, turned, and returned to his car.

Cami's eyes narrowed. "I'd watch my back if I were you."

"Yeah, well, it's not my back that's hurting. I think I've got a broken rib."

She grimaced.

It felt good to have her so close. To feel her hot breath against my flesh. Hope springs eternal, I mused.

With her support, we reached my car and she helped me get in. After inspecting my face in the interior light, her forehead wrinkled empathetically. "Let's get back to your apartment and I'll patch you up. Maybe by morning, you'll be up to traveling."

"Traveling? But what about Lily? We've got to start looking for her," I protested.

Nodding, she continued, "Trace, whoever took Lily has a huge lead on us. Plus, we have no idea which direction they went." Softening her tone, she whispered, "She's in God's hands now. Even if we caught up with them, you're in no shape to help her. Now, I need to get you patched up. Tomorrow we'll start all over."

Releasing a weak sigh, I pulled the envelope Detective Ashcroft found. I opened it and pulled out a picture. It was the one I found on Peterson's desk when I searched for the files.

Holding it to the light, I studied it with interest. "I know this place."

Cami leaned in to get a better look. Her hot breath wafted around me like a soft summer breeze. "You do? Where is it?"

"I've seen it in a magazine. It's a ski lodge up in Squaw Valley. Peterson must have had his picture taken there recently. Look, that's his car in the background. Plus, his car was missing when we found Peterson's body. I'll bet you that's where the guy is headed."

Cami's face contorted. "How do you know that?"

"When I searched Peterson's office, I saw a map next to the picture. It's got to be where they're going."

"They have about a five hour lead and it's late. I personally don't want to be driving up those winding roads at this time of night."

I had to agree with her. I was in no condition to save anyone.

With effort, I tucked the picture into my pocket. Every movement caused my head to throb. "We should at least call the local police and ask them to be on the lookout for them."

Cami grabbed her cell phone and hit a button.

"Who are you calling?"

"I have a better idea," she said and held up a finger for him to be quiet. "Hello, Jason? Sorry to wake you. Is the chopper available tomorrow?" She nodded and smiled. "Good for you. At the ready, we'll be there at six-thirty in the morning."

I stared ahead. "Did I just hear you book a flight on the governor's helicopter?"

"Candidate Sanchez's chopper to be more accurate, and yes. Now let's get a move on. I'll meet you at your apartment. Tomorrow we'll go for a ride."

The drive back to my apartment gave me time to think, to pray. The thought of Lily being in the hands of a killer chilled me to the core. *Oh Lord, put a hedge of protection around my little girl.* As I drove, I punched in Ron's number. He answered on the first ring.

"Ron here. Whatcha need?"

I grinned at my friend's willingness to serve no matter the hour. "I need you to get the guys praying. My daughter Lily is in some kind of trouble. I need God to put his hand of protection around her."

"You got it, buddy. Where are you now?"

"Don't worry, I'm not anywhere near a bar."

Ron's boisterous laughter filled the connection. "Okay, buddy. Just checking."

I ended the call more confident than I'd been in a long time.

When we reached my apartment, I eased from behind the wheel and stood. A wave of nausea followed by lightheadedness washed over me. Before I toppled over, Cami was at my side. Her arm snaked around me and hauled me upright. With her support, we made it to my door. While I fidgeted with the lock, Wag bounded for the first tree in sight.

"Dogs will be dogs," Cami said, waiting for him to return.

I gave her a weak shrug. "If I don't get inside soon, I might have to follow his example."

Cami shook her head in a typical womanly fashion. The way she looked at me, made me wonder if it was more than just concern for another human being? Had the old flames of our charred relationship been rekindled? Could she love a man with my past? Could I let this woman into my shattered heart? And then there was the matter of her spiritual condition. I was a believer … she wasn't. As a believer, I couldn't violate my conscience or what I knew the Bible said. Closing my eyes, I sent up a quick prayer for God to change her heart because as far as I was concerned, mine could not be trusted.

In the background, I heard Cami clearing her throat. "Let's get you inside and see to your lip and eye. That will be a real shiner by tomorrow."

Once inside, I tried not to play the wounded soldier part too much but secretly enjoyed her closeness. After she finished doctoring me up, she disappeared into the bathroom and returned with a glass of water, a handful of pills, and a blanket.

"Here, take these and don't call me in the morning," an impish glint danced in her eyes.

"What? Are you going to leave me here alone in my weakened condition with that beast of a dog?"

Shaking her head, she clipped Wag's leash. "No, I thought about it, but five-thirty comes mighty early. I'll sleep in your bedroom. You share the couch with Wag. Good night. I'm beat."

With a quick turn, she sauntered down the hall and disappeared.

Too sore to move, I stretched out on the couch, tugged a blanket over my shoulders. As I drifted off to sleep, two faces played across my eyes … Lily's … and Cami's.

Chapter Thirty-Four

The sound of jangling keys in my front door brought me to an upright position.

It was in moments like this I wished I had a gun. As of yet, I did not. My concealed carry license was hung up somewhere in the bureaucratic quagmire. And since I lived in one of the most restrictive states in the country, when it came to gun ownership, I wondered if I'd ever get one.

Grabbing a scissors from the coffee table, I prepared to defend myself when I realized it was just Cami returning from walking Wag.

I barely had time to hide the scissors when two large paws pounced on my chest. Wag's hot breath engulfed me. His slobbery tongue licked away any notion I had of sleep.

"Okay, okay, I'm awake already." I tried to move, but every muscle in my body screamed in protest.

"Wag, let him alone." Cami's chuckling voice rang in my ears. It was something I could get used to. "How do you feel?" Her question interrupted my machinations.

Stifling a yawn, I shoved Wag aside and tried to stretch.

He yawned and stretched too. Like master, like dog. I just hoped I didn't look like him. Then again, knowing his luck with the lady dogs, maybe that wasn't such a bad thing.

"Like I've been hit by a truck," I uttered at length.

Cami finished adding more coffee grounds to yesterday's batch, flipped it on and grabbed two coffee mugs.

I cringed.

After living together for two years, she knew how I felt about reusing coffee grounds. "Did I just see you add grounds to yesterday's coffee? That is worse than secondhand smoke, or watching a 'B' rated movie two times in a row."

"Quit complaining and get dressed," she said kiddingly. "We're going for a ride in the governor's helicopter."

I groaned at the thought. Flying was one of my least favorite things to do, especially taking off and landing. With care, I eased to a standing position and hobbled to the bathroom. I hoped a hot shower would loosen up my knotted muscles.

Twenty minutes later, I emerged feeling like a new man. Towel drying my hair, I reentered the galley kitchen where a fresh mug of coffee awaited me.

"You read my mind."

"I read your face." She inhaled the fresh soapy scent and smiled.

"Much better." Tossing me a bagel, Cami finished hers and rinsed out her mug. "That will hold me till lunchtime."

I finished wolfing down my breakfast, set the plate in the sink and reached for my coat. "Oh!"

A pained expression came over Cami's face. "Here, let me help you." With her assistance, I laced up my hiking boots, slipped on my overcoat while she zipped up hers.

"You look so much better than you did last night," eying my bruises. "It's too bad I didn't send Wag with you. He would have given those guys a run for their money."

"Or died trying," I added ruefully, rubbing the black lab.

$$$

At five-thirty in the morning, the western sky was a deep ebony punctuated with glittering specks of silver.

Golden splashes of light seeped between the eastern mountain peaks painting the wispy clouds in soft pastel tones. The snow-covered crests caught some of the rays and were transformed into blazing cliffs of amber.

Using Cami's vehicle, we made the drive across town in less than thirty minutes. As she turned the last corner, a shaft of sunlight stung her eyes. Squinting she yanked down the sun visor but even then, some of the glare reflected off the hood making it hard to see. She tapped the brake lightly, slowing the car as she entered the tarmac. Ahead, sitting on a chopper pad, was the governor's private helicopter. She brought the car as close as she dared and killed the engine.

"Good, he's got her ready to go."

With care, I unfolded myself from the passenger's side and limped around to open the door for Cami. By the time I got there, she had already bolted out and was inspecting the chopper.

By now, the props of the four-seater were slowly spinning. Cami ducked and scampered to the pilot. "Hey Jason, thanks for the lift. We have a real emergency. We need to be up at Squaw Valley Ski Resort el-quicko."

Jason, wiping his hands on an oily rag, eyed me and Wag with suspicion. "Who are your guests?"

Cami grew serious. "Oh that's Wag, and, and" she paused. "He's my friend, Trace O'Reilly."

Jason pocketed the rag and stuck out his hand. "Oh, you're the guy who nearly got it in the neck. I thought that was you. It's nice to meet you." He rung my hand vigorously. "And for the record; I didn't think you were guilty."

His chuckle was refreshing. "Thanks, Jason. Neither did I."

With a nod, the pilot climbed into the cockpit and glanced over his shoulder. "Well, hop in, put on your headphones, fasten your safety harnesses, and get ready for the ride of your life."

I didn't like the sound of that, but complied.

As we took our seats and followed his instruction, the pilot wound up the turbines. A sudden jerk and we were airborne. Instinctively, I grabbed the first solid thing within arm's length. The problem was, everything was moving. First up, then forward. I felt the bagel crawling up my throat and willed it back down. Cami and Wag seemed to be taking the sudden roller-coaster ride in stride. Not so with me.

Feeling slightly lightheaded, I closed my eyes and prayed the landing would be smoother than the takeoff.

Twenty minutes into the flight, we were skimming across the tops of the foothills, headed for the ski lodge.

"Uh, oh, we've got a problem," Jason's voice crackled in our headsets. I glanced over his shoulder. He was gripping the vibrating control stick with both.

"What's wrong?" Cami asked, her voice ratcheting up a notch.

Jason pointed his nose in the direction of a large cloud mass. "That spells trouble for a helicopter. We're going to have to put down somewhere out of the wind and ride it out."

"We can't," I hollered through the comm. "We have an emergency and need to get to the lodge."

Cami clutched the seat as the chopper hit an air pocket. The sudden drop in altitude sent Wag upward until the straps holding him snapped taut. His eyes widened and he let out a fearful yelp.

"No can do, those winds will tear us apart."

I leaned forward. "You don't understand. There is a man holding a hostage in the lodge and we are going there to negotiate her release. The young woman is my daughter. If we don't get there soon, he's going to kill her." Most of which was true, but I was desperate.

"What about the police? Can't we call them?"

"I have," Cami answered, "The small police force in Squaw Valley has been reassigned to cover a multi-car accident on the highway. They won't make it there in time. We're his daughter's only hope."

The pilot clinched his teeth, set his jaw and bore down on the throttle. "Mr. O'Reilly, I've got a daughter too, and I would do anything for her. I'll get you up that mountain if it kills me."

His resolve reminded me of Rose Beretta's question. 'Would you do *anything* to save your family?' It was obvious this pilot had the answer. I was still working on mine.

The feeble aircraft shuddered forward as the storm closed in around it. In the blinding white-out conditions, the pilot had to rely on his instruments to maintain control.

"I can't see a hundred feet ahead of me," Cami said, looking more frightened than I'd ever seen her.

"I know, at this rate, we could fly into the side of the mountain," the pilot hollered into the comm.

"How much farther?" Cami asked, her knuckles white as she clung to the seat, her breath coming in short gasps.

Jason glanced at the spinning gages. "Another ten minutes, but—"

The helicopter jolted as one of its skids clipped a rocky outcropping. The helicopter began to spin out of control. Jason yanked back on the yoke to counter the spin. In the upper atmosphere, the winds tore at the small aircraft with claw-like ferocity.

"We're losing her," he yelled, as the helicopter took a nosedive toward a field of pristine white.

Holding back on the stick, Jason fought to bring the aircraft down, but a gust of wind caught it at the last second and flipped it on its side. The prop struck a boulder, throwing the small fuselage upside down. The nose plowed into a snow bank and jolted to a stop. Cami, Wag and I were thrown around like two rag-dolls.

Then everything went black.

Chapter Thirty-Five

I'm not sure how long we hung by our seat restraints. Long enough for the cold to claw through the outer shell of the broken helicopter and penetrate my thin coat.

Her lips blue from the biting cold, Cami shivered … her eyelids but slits. All at once, she sucked in a sharp breath and roused. "Where's Jason?" She screamed getting my full attention.

The pilot's side door had been ripped open and hung by one hinge. Blood splatters marked the frame. A bloody trail marked the trajectory his body had taken as he was flung from the aircraft.

"He's gone! The prop must have struck him as we rolled." I hated to be so matter-of-fact, but time was running out.

With moments to spare, I unsnapped my safety harness and eased my body down. Taking Cami by the shoulders, I released her restraint and help her get her footing. "Let's get out of here before this thing blows."

Grabbing Wag by the collar and Cami by the hand, I tugged them through the drifting snow. We dove behind a snowdrift just as the tanks ruptured. In an instant, the helicopter was engulfed in flames. Shards of metal flew in every direction and rained down around us.

Cami yelped. "My leg!"

Glancing down, I saw a shard of metal protruding from her thigh. Crimson blood oozed through her pants and stained the snow. The seriousness of our situation hit me with full-force. We were two miles from the lodge, ill-prepared for hiking, injured, and caught in a violent ice storm.

She moaned. Her face was the color of the surrounding snow, her lips paled, her breathing grew shallow.

This was all my fault. I was too stubborn to get the authorities involved. Why hadn't I trusted the system? I knew why. The system failed me too many times. But that didn't assuage the guilt which gnawed at me like a cancer.

Cami's icy hand gripped mine rousing my senses back.

"I'm going to see if the first-aid kit survived the explosion."

Cami didn't respond.

As I tried to get her comfortable, Wag came over and laid next to her.

"Good boy, keep her warm until I get back." Bracing against the blinding snow, I pushed through the storm until I reached the smoldering wreckage.

Lord, help me find the first-aid kit. My frozen lips barely moved, but my heart burned with urgency.

After a few minutes of rummaging, I found a white box with a red cross painted on its lid and a foil blanket. Struggling against the biting wind which threatened to blow my feet out from under me, I followed my trail back to where I left Cami. She was shaking violently.

"She's going into shock," I muttered to Wag. The dog nuzzled her with his nose trying to get a response.

There was none.

My heart stuttered.

You're a jerk for putting Cami and the pilot's lives in jeopardy, I chided myself.

But what about Lily? Her life matters too, my better-self countered. In that moment, I'd made up my mind. I was willing to do whatever it took to save my family. That didn't assuage the guilt eating away at my soul for putting Jason and Cami's life on the line. I knew I couldn't do anything for the pilot, but I was determined to do everything in my power to save Lily and Cami. Wrapping the insulated blanket around her, I kept a steady eye on the wound.

"Okay, Wag. You keep her warm while I look at Cami's leg." The dog seemed to understand and crawled closer.

"Cami, can you hear me?"

She roused.

"I need you to lay still and let me inspect your leg."

She nodded, gritting her teeth.

It wasn't hard to find the piece of metal which had struck her. However, getting it out was the problem. Taking care not to make her suffering any worse, I tore open Cami's pant leg and inspected the bloody wound.

"It looks worse than it is." I tried to put a brave face on a bad situation.

"It feels worse than it looks," Cami slurred.

Scooping up a handful of snow, I packed the gash, hoping to numb it. "That should help until I can think what to do next."

The icy crystals froze my fingers, and I blew on them in an attempt to restore feeling.

It didn't work.

Being careful not to do any more damage to the wound, I eased the shard out. Breathing easier, I repacked it with more snow. Thankfully, the metal hadn't cut an artery.

"Why did you hesitate when Jason asked who I was?" trying to get Cami's mind off her leg.

Cami bit her lip and looked down at the wrapping.

"For a moment, I thought about lying." Her candor took me by surprise.

I nodded. "It's a good thing you didn't. Jason would have called you on it."

A weak smile parted Cami's lips. "Yeah, you're right."

Cami lifted herself to one elbow. "The other day, when I was drilling you about getting 'religion,'" she paused and wiped a tear. "Some of the things you said made sense. You see, I may look like I have it all together, but in reality, I don't. Ever since we broke up and even before that, my life was a wreck. I knew it and more than that, God knew it. He's been chasing me all my life and I've been running from Him. What you said about finding something you couldn't find in a bottle; well, that made sense to me. I wasn't an alcoholic like you, but I was a workaholic. I thought the more I worked, the more fulfilled I'd be."

"And?"

"All I got for my trouble was an ulcer, more work, and a deep emptiness."

"So what did I say that helped you?" I asked, as I finished dressing the wound.

"It wasn't exactly what you said, but how you said it. Your genuineness cut through all my arguments. I had an old pamphlet someone had given me at the grocery store. I rooted it from my purse and read it over and over." Tears rolled down her cheeks, unhindered.

I waited for Cami to gain her composure. I wanted more than anything to lift her to my chest and hold her but knew it would send the wrong message.

Finally, Cami took a cleansing breath. "In simple terms, I did as you did. I put my trust in Jesus and gave Him control of my life. I was going to tell you, but this," looking over her shoulder at the crumpled shell of the helicopter, "that happened."

Extending my arms, I pulled her into a firm embrace. I felt her throbbing heart and for a moment, they beat in unison. God had answered my prayer. The warmth of her breath on my neck caused my heart to skip.

"You don't know how many times I prayed for this moment, but thought it would never happen, especially as they were wheeling me to the … " my throat closed as a fresh round of tears streamed from my eyes. "Cami," I said, pulling away from her grasp.

"—not now Trace. Let's get through this and then you can—"

I waved her off. "I wasn't going to say what you think I was going to say. What I was going to say was, I need to see if I can salvage something from the wreckage I could use to make a sled."

"A sled ... Are you crazy? We've lost, can't you see?" pointing to her leg.

"I've got to try. That's my daughter up there."

Standing, I pushed through the storm. Billows of black smoke swirled in the wind, making it difficult to see. Knowing time was running out, I pried loose one of the stabilizers and a skid from the helicopter's landing gear. Using a couple of metal stays for ski poles, I built a makeshift sled. After tying the safety harnesses together, I looked at Wag who'd patiently watched me with interest.

"Okay, buddy, how's your mushing skills? Wag cocked his head."

"I take it that means we're good to go." As I spoke, I eased Cami on the skid, then tied her down to keep her from slipping off.

Once I was certain of that, I returned to the crash site and found the pilot's body.

"What are you doing?" Cami asked, her voice weak.

"It's called surviving." Careful not to desecrate the pilot's broken, half snow-covered body, I slid his jacket off of him and jammed my arms through the sleeves.

"Okay, hold on. We're going for a ride."

Chapter Thirty-Six

A single figure stepped from a car in front of the Alpine Ski Resort.

Within seconds, he was covered with a layer of wet snow. Shielding his face to keep the snow from blinding him, Nelson tugged the hood of his coat over his head and drew the string tight. His actions, however, did little to keep frost from forming on his face and nose.

The early winter storm, which visited the Alpine Ski Resort in Squaw Valley near Lake Tahoe, temporarily delayed his arrival. Now he stood and braced himself against the icy wind which blew through the canyon.

Driving through the blizzard all night left him bone weary, and he ached all over, but he finally pushed his vehicle through the snow-covered mountain roads and arrived safe and sound. The only evidence of his passage was two deep ravines which cut through the otherwise pristine snow. It would only be a matter of minutes before the tracks disappeared underneath a fresh layer of snow.

"This wasn't the way I planned it, but it will work. It is the perfect place for a wedding and a honeymoon." He chuckled wickedly at himself.

The idea of killing his brother, and staging it to look like Trace O'Reilly did it, was a stroke of genius. While

Trace and that woman broke into Nate's upstairs office, he'd slipped out and stole the tire tool from Trace's car. It wasn't hard to do. Using a screwdriver, he popped the trunk open. A second later he had what he needed. Fortunately, he had the foresight to carry a handkerchief insuring he'd left no incriminating fingerprints. With Nate out of the way, he planned on maintaining his brother's identity until the estate was settled.

That was the plan and it was a good one.

Yes, indeed, he mused … a very good plan.

The deserted village lay under a thick blanket of heavy snow giving it a magical appearance. Not even a skeleton crew had ventured up the mountain leaving the resort completely deserted, except for him and his new bride-to-be.

His shoes scrunched the snow beneath them as he surveyed the scene but he couldn't stay there. A cold wind sliced through his outer garment sending a chill down his back. With a sigh, he pulled his coat closer. When he reached the rear of the car, he popped the trunk lid open.

Inside, wrapped in several thick blankets was Lily, her limp body offered him no resistance as he lifted her in his arms. With care, he carried her up the icy steps onto the broad veranda. Snow had drifted in long, rippled piles up to the windows. Fortunately, the front doors were shielded allowing him to approach it without slipping.

"Let's get you inside, my dear, where you can warm up," he whispered in her ear. Her head lolled to the side unresponsively.

He gave the front door a swift kick and it flew open. Being careful not to strike her head on the doorframe, he carried her over the thresh-hold. A wicked smile stretched across his face. He set the unconscious girl on the floor and returned to the car for their two suitcases. Returning, he closed the door behind him, and locked it, hoping no one had seen him. He fingered the gun in his pocket.

If they did, he'd be ready.

Then he turned his attention to the front desk. Scanning the rows of keys, his eyes locked on the one marked Honeymoon Suite. Barely able to contain his anticipation, he lifted the key and returned to the unconscious girl.

With care, he lifted her in his arms. Her head lolled against his shoulder and he pulled her tight.

"Only a few more minutes and you'll be mine … all mine," he whispered. Turning, he began climbing the long, winding staircase up to the second floor where the bridal suite awaited them.

After making all the preparations, he sat back and waited for the drugs he'd given Lily to wear off. Finally, after an hour, Lily's mind cleared and she lifted her head.

$$$

The night before, while the drugs Nelson had given her were beginning to take effect, Lily heard voices downstairs.

Angry voices. It was her step-dad and his brother and they were arguing. As the two men's tempers flared it was clear, the scene would turn ugly. Fear gripped Lily's heart and squeezed the air from her lungs. Her head felt heavy, but she wanted to listen. Laying back on her bed, she allowed sleep to enfold her.

As the drugs took over, she drifted but not so much that she was not aware of the two powerful arms which carried her. First, they laid her in a dark place and covered her with blankets. After drifting in and out, she felt the movement stop and was blinded by daylight. Snow swirled around her and she inhaled icy air.

She roused, but only for a second.

Again, those two arms hoisted her up and carried her into a warm room. Still feeling the effects of the drugs, she let herself fade in and out of sleep.

"Where am I?" Lily muttered. Her confused brain tried to focus but refused to fully grasp her situation.

With her hands tied to the arms of a wooden chair, and her feet bound, she sat immobilized, staring back at two lust-filled eyes … Nelson Peterson's eyes.

The man straightened and inspected his work. "You are in our honeymoon suite and you are about to become my bride."

Her mind cleared instantly.

"What? Why? I don't understand."

"Oh, I think you do, my dear. How could you not know? I've loved you ever since you came into my life. And now I want to spend it with you. My brother, God rest his soul, was poisoning you. That's why you were always sick, but I caught him. I made him pay for his sin."

Lily's breath caught in her throat.

Nelson's eyes grew distant, then refocused. "Now you will repay me by becoming my wife." His voice quivered with excitement.

The cords binding her wrists and ankles dug into her skin as she strained against them. "You'll never get away with this," she spat. "I will never love you. You're crazy if you think I do."

"Now, now Lily, don't say something you will regret. Today should be a happy day, a day of celebration." His eyes danced with glee.

"Say what?"

"Don't you remember, it's your twenty-first birthday and," he flipped over a full-length mirror, "it's your wedding day."

The color leaked from her face as she stared in horror at the pure white wedding gown clinging to her.

"Noooo!" she cried, struggling to free herself.

Nelson's wolfish grin faded, "Oh honey, don't do that. Not in your weakened condition."

She slumped back into the chair, her head swimming. "I feel sick."

"Yes, and you should. You're not at all well, and haven't been for quite some time, thanks to my wicked brother. But I have saved you."

Handing her a scrap of paper, he continued, "Here, read this over several times. When you are ready, I want you to read it with feeling."

Her fingers trembled as she took the proffered sheet. She studied it for a second and felt terror rumble through her stomach.

"This is a wedding vow, I'm not reading this." She let the paper fall from her fingers. It slid quietly to the floor.

Peterson bent over to pick it up. As he did, Lily kicked him with all her might. As if in slow motion, he toppled over. In an instant, he was upon her. His powerful hands clamped around her throat and squeezed. The air in her lungs cried desperately for release and the room tilted. Then he relaxed his grip and straightened. A wicked smile curled his lips.

"Well, it's not unusual for newlyweds to have a spat. Consider it our first. Now, if you will kindly practice reading this, at exactly noon, we will be man and wife," he said, his tone conciliatory.

She spit in his face. Before she could duck, his hand flew back and struck her across the face. "Consider that our second, and last." He glared at her, his eyes wild.

An angry welt formed on her cheek and she bit back her tears. "I'll never read that stupid vow," spitting blood from her cut lip.

"Oh, you will read it, and then you'll sign this document," he said, pointing to her Last Will and Testament. "And this," he waved his hand in an arc, "will be our love-nest. Don't you just love it?"

Lily glowered at him. "No, never!"

A mirthless laugh that didn't reach his eyes percolated in his throat. "I like a girl with spunk."

Eyes widening, she watched him pull a syringe from his pocket. Turning the tip upward, he flicked it with his fingers and pushed the plunger until a narrow stream of clear liquid sprayed out. Muscles tensing, Lily pulled back as far as possible but she couldn't move far enough.

His eyes danced excitedly as he jabbed the tip into her arm. Then he forced the fluid into her vein and stepped back.

It only took a second for her head to tilt heavily to one side. Her stomach roiled and she let out a slurred curse.

"There, that's not so bad. Soon you will feel better. It's too bad we will not grow old together. As luck would have it, you will have an unfortunate accident on the ski slopes."

"No, no, no, noo," she slurred.

"Oh yes, I can see it now. Tomorrow's headline will read, 'Honeymoon ends in tragedy. Lily Peterson dies in a fluke skiing accident.' Don't you just love it?"

Again, a muffled 'no' escaped her lips.

"Oh, and by the way, I believe congratulations are in order. As of a few minutes ago, you became a millionaire. But alas, you aren't going to enjoy a penny of it."

Taking her hand in his, he forced her to sign the Marriage License and Last Will and Testament. Then he added his own signature.

"Now, Lily, do you take this man to be your lawfully wedded husband?"

She lifted her head and muttered something incoherent.

"I'll take that as a 'yes.'"

He pulled a sheet of paper from his pocket and read, "I, Nate Peterson, do take thee, Lily Peterson, as my lawfully wedded wife. I will love you and keep you until death do we part." As he leaned over to kiss her, she lurched forward and head-butted him, cutting his lip. He spat the blood from his mouth with a curse.

"Okay, now for the grand finale."

Chapter Thirty-Seven

"Wag, come here, boy," I called over the howling wind.

He eagerly pushed through the snow to where I knelt. The harness, which I'd tied to the skid fit snuggly to his furry coat. I cinched it as tight as I dared and made sure the knot connecting it to the make-shift sleigh was secure.

After rechecking the ropes which held Cami to the sled, I brushed aside a few strands of hair from her forehead, leaned down and kissed her. "Tell me if this is too tight. I don't want you to go falling off halfway up that mountain."

Cami grimaced. "No, it's not. I just hope it works, and I'm not frozen like a Popsicle when we get to the top."

I rechecked the linkage, stepped on the rear of the sleigh, and smiled. "I always thought you were a pretty cool girl, now I'll find out how cool."

That said, I gave the reins a quick jerk and Wag began pulling the skid with all his might.

"We're making better time than I thought," Cami called through a blanket of snow, which had gathered on her chest.

I tried to answer, but my face felt like it had been chiseled into a block of ice. My one hand, now frozen in place, gripped the ski pole while the other held the rope leading to Wag. Great puffs of condensation coursed from the dog as he put his heart in the effort.

Peering ahead, I caught a glimpse of the road and guided the sleigh toward it. Fortunately, a line of trees on the windward side kept the snow from piling up and it became easier to navigate.

With effort, Wag pulled the skid through the snow-pack until his feet were encrusted with ice. His coat glistened with frozen sweat and muggy snow. He slowed his pace and began to cough up blood. Seeing the dog's condition deteriorating, my heart dipped.

"Cami, I'm so sorry. I don't think Wag is going to make it."

Not getting an answer, I looked at Cami. Her arms were crossed, her chin buried in her chest and she looked like a snow mummy. Her face showed early signs of frostbite. The pain of seeing my two friends dying was nearly unbearable. Trudging forward, I knelt and took Wag by the head and rubbed it.

"Look Wag, ole buddy. I know this is a lot to ask of you, but we gotta make it up that mountain. My daughter is up there and an evil man may be taking advantage of her." Looking over my shoulder, I forced out the words. "Plus, Cami," I took a dry swallow. "Cami is dying. We gotta get her to a warm place. So, I beg you. Try just a little bit more and I promise to take care of you and help you get well. But please, help me save Cami. Help me save my daughter."

Struggling to his feet, Wag prepared to take a step but his legs buckled.

My heart sank.

This is not good … not ... at … all.

Hope slipped and I bowed my head.

"Lord, we need you. I know I haven't been the best example of a Christian, but I've been trying. Cami just became a believer, and I sure would like to see her come to know the joy you've given me. So could you help Wag pull us up this mountain?"

All at once, Wag pushed himself to his feet and shook. Pellets of mud and icy water flew in concentric circles pelting me in the face. Barely able to stand, I straightened. I had been kneeling so long, that my legs refused to move. Gritting my teeth, I forced my frozen hands to grab the sled as Wag tugged it forward.

A few minutes later, the lodge appeared in the distance.

Chapter Thirty-Eight

K nowing her life was in mortal danger, Lily fought to stay alert.

As Peterson untied her, she lifted her leg and kicked. Her foot landed squarely in his groin. He groaned, buckled, and hit the floor, gasping for air.

Before he could recover, she wobbled to her feet and staggered to the door.

One more step and she would have made it, but his hand caught her ankle, tripping her, sending her sprawling. As she fell, she knocked over an end table with an old fashioned telephone on it.

In an instant, Peterson was upon her, pinning her shoulders to the floor.

She twisted under his weight, but it was too much.

A wicked grin spread across his face, and she knew the evil which awaited her if she didn't act fast.

Hands flailing, she searched for something she could use to defend her honor. Her fingers touched the old phone and closed around it. Gritting her teeth, she swung, striking him on the side of the head.

Peterson swayed and fell forward. As he did, his head came in contact with the corner of the table. For a moment, Lily laid still, panting, too weak to move. The pungent aroma of his aftershave attacked her senses, gagging her, choking her, causing her stomach to churn. As Peterson's weight pressed down upon her, she fought to breathe.

Then, everything went dark.

$$$

As the lodge came into view, the blood in my veins turned to ice.

Nate's car sat in front of the lodge. Its trunk and side passenger door stood open. Snow piled inside. Had that beast violated my daughter? Had he killed her? Was I too late? Questions fluttered through my mind like a flock of angry birds.

Feeling a surge of adrenaline, I willed the sled forward. With Wag's strength flagging, and the added weight from the snow collecting on Cami's body, the sled bogged down into every snow drift. Fear gripped my heart at the thought that I'd not only lost my daughter but lost Cami and Wag.

In desperation, I made my way to the front of the sled. Lifting Wag to my shoulders, I grabbed the reigns and plunged ahead.

My injuries screamed in protest with every ponderous step, but I kept going. Nearly exhausted, I reached the steps and pounded up them. As gently as possible, I laid Wag down on the porch and threw myself against the doors. They shattered scattering glass and chips of wood across the tiled floor. Forgetting my frozen hands, I grabbed the front of the sled and tugged it inside.

With his legs barely able to support him, Wag dragged himself in and flopped on an area rug in front of a large fireplace. His breathing was shallow and I thought I'd lost him. "Hang in there Wag, I'm coming."

Torn between saving Lily or Cami and Wag, my mind screamed for a decision. *Who do I save first, God!*

In an instant, I recognized what Wag had done. To the right of the fireplace was a stack of cured wood. I tossed several logs into the hearth and began to search for some matches. On the mantle lay a box of matches. With trembling fingers, I pulled one out and struck it, then lit the gas-jets. A moment later, the flame caught hold and began to crawl from log to log sending heat throughout the lobby.

Wasting no time, I scraped the snow and ice from Cami's outer clothes, untied her and laid her as close to the open fire as I dared. Then I leaned down and whispered in Wag's ear, "Good dog, you got us here, now I'm going to take care of you."

Carefully, I laid him close to Cami. After seeing to the needs of my friends, my thoughts turned to Lily.

I glanced around and realized how large the lodge was. "I wonder where he could have taken her."

The front desk located on the other side of the lobby drew my attention. I pushed myself up on shaky legs and staggered around the counter to where a pegboard occupied the wall.

A sick feeling squirreled through my gut.

He's taken her to the bridal suite.

Next to the pegboard was a floor plan of the lodge. After taking a moment to study the layout, I sprang for the stairs. By now, my legs had regained some of their strength and I dashed to the second floor taking two steps at a time. Down the hall I plunged, scanning the numbers as I went.

With the door to the bridal suite in my sights, I lowered my shoulder and smashed into it. It splintered, sending chunks of wood flying and it sprang back. My momentum carried me into the center of the room. Head on a swivel, I scanned the area.

She wasn't in the living room. I heard rustling in the next room and slammed through the bedroom door. Lily lay on the bed, her hands and feet were tied to the four corner posts. Her eyes were widened with terror as Nelson Peterson leaned over her. He turned to face me as a wicked grin faded into a sneer.

The man was insane with lustful thoughts.

"You—"

Before Nelson could react, I dove for him, knocking him off the bed, onto the floor. My hands closed around his neck. I had one thought … kill him.

Nelson broke my hold and landed a solid punch to my jaw. Stunned, I fell back giving him just enough time to crawl out from under me. Using his six foot frame, he angled himself into position and lunged at me.

I shifted, allowing his weight to throw him off balance. He landed hard on a coffee table, smashing it into pieces and sending burning candles across the floor.

The flames caught hold of the lacy curtains and crawled upward. Ignoring the new threat, Peterson sprang to his feet and lunged for a gun which sat on an end table.

His fingers closed around the butt and he swung around. Leveling the barrel, he squeezed the trigger.

I ducked as the weapon discharged.

The bullet struck a mirror, sending shards of glass to the floor. Not regarding the damage it would do to my fingers, I picked up a ten-inch piece of glass and threw it like a knife. It sliced through the air like a missile and stuck Peterson's chest. He cursed and yanked it out. Blood seeped from the wound, leaving a crimson streak on his white shirt.

Smoke began to fill the bridal suite, blinding me.

Again, Peterson lifted the weapon and took aim.

I zigged.

He followed my movements, but didn't fire lest he strike Lily.

I zagged, grabbed the broken table leg and swung. The wood struck his wrist, knocking the weapon free.

He groaned.

The gun fell from his grip and skittered across the floor.

Smoke stung my eyes as the air grew acrid.

Driven by desperation we both dove for the weapon. My fingers were the first to touch it, but in the blinding smoke, it danced further from my grip.

Feeling the effects of the beating I'd received previous night and exertion from trying to get here, I knew if I didn't do something fast, I would lose everything. I struggled to my feet and leaped over a couch, putting distance between him and me.

Think, think, think! I tried to clear the lightheadedness that invaded my head.

I needed a better weapon.

Before I could react, Nelson leaped over the couch knocking me backward. My back hit a set of double doors leading to the outside balcony, smashing them open.

Outside, the storm raged on.

Like shrapnel, icy pellets rained down upon me as I skidded against the railing.

In a flash, Peterson was on me, his hands clamping like a vise on my throat. He grinned wickedly and began to squeeze.

Everything got real quiet. His face seemed miles away as my lungs screamed for oxygen.

A dull thud sounded in the distance and Peterson's grip loosened. Air seeped into my lungs and I realized what had happened. Taking advantage of the moment, I broke Nelson's hold on me and jammed my thumb into his right eye.

He cursed.

As he tumbled to one side, I caught a glimpse of Cami. She stood, two white knuckled hands gripped the butt of the gun. A slight wisp of smoke drifted from its barrel.

The distraction was all Nelson needed. Driven by hatred and adrenaline, he lunged forward. Another bullet exploded from the gun striking Peterson in the shoulder, spinning him around, and sending him over the railing.

Time hesitated as Nelson clung to the icy railing. His feet kicked wildly, searching for a foothold, anything to keep from falling. One by one, his fingers peeled back, and he tumbled into the darkness.

I forced my legs under me and stood.
Gasping for air, I peered over the railing.
A crimson trail marked Peterson's escape.

Chapter Thirty-Nine

Still holding the gun, Cami stared blankly.

"He's getting away," she said.

As her grip on the weapon weakened, she wobbled and dropped it. It fell with a heavy thud.

By now, the fire had creeped across the ceiling and was licking at the canopy covered bed. I filled my lungs with fresh air and plunged into the room just as Cami's knees buckled. Grasping her, I lowered her to the floor.

"He won't get far, not in this storm. Look Cami, I need you to crawl into the hall. Do you think you can do that?"

She nodded bravely.

"I thought I'd lost you there for a minute," she said as a coughing spell overtook her.

"I thought the same thing but you need to get yourself and Wag to safety … now!"

She forced her stiff legs to obey her and dragged herself away from the flaming danger.

I wrapped my hand with a towel, grabbed a jagged piece of mirror and sliced the ropes which bound Lily to the bed. Then I scooped her in my arms and carried her into the hall.

After closing the splintered door to keep the fire from reaching us, I checked Lily's pupils.

"She's in shock," I muttered.

As I attended to the two women, Wag limped into view. He drew near to where Lily lay and licked her cheek. She stirred, and let out a weak moan. She tried to speak, but her words were slurred.

Cami leaned over Lily's limp form and checked her pupils. "We need to get her to the hospital as fast as possible."

"Peterson's car is out front. Let's use it," I said.

Being careful not to jostle her too much, I lifted Lily up and ran down to the first floor.

Cami pushed herself to her feet and limped down the hall behind me with Wag close behind, his bloody paws leaving crimson prints with each labored step. They reached the car just as I laid Lily in the back seat and fastened the seatbelt.

After helping Cami get into the passenger's side, I turned to Wag. "Don't worry, ol' buddy, I'm not leaving without you." I lifted him and placed him next to Cami.

Once they were secure, I hobbled around to the driver's side. With every labored step, my bruised muscles and joints protested. I settled in behind the wheel and noticed the key was still in the ignition where Nelson, in his haste, had left them.

"Thank you, Lord," I said.

As cold as it was outside, it took several tries to get the engine to turn over. With the snow still piling up, I found it quite difficult to get the big vehicle to move. After rocking the car back and forth, I was able to get enough momentum to roll over the mounds of snow and get the car moving in the right direction. As I nursed it down the mountain, Cami laid her head back and stroked Wag's matted fur.

"I heard you talking to Wag and praying, and I knew I had to make it. If you hadn't gotten me to that fireplace, I wouldn't have lasted another ten minutes."

I took a dry swallow. "Wag saved our lives, you know?"

Cami tilted her head up and considered me for a moment. "You and Wag saved our lives."

$$$

In nearly white-out conditions, the journey was painfully slow.

Several times the car skittered sideways and I had to fight to keep it from going over the railing.

"Trace, we're losing her. Can you go any faster?" Cami said, after rechecking Lily's vitals.

Squinting to see ahead, I gripped the steering wheel. "I'm making my best time. Talk to her, try to keep her alert."

Being careful not to reinjure her leg, Cami crawled into the backseat and leaned close to her ear. An old song percolated from her throat. It must have been one she'd learned as a little girl because it flowed so easily from her lips.

From time to time, Lily would open her eyes and gaze past Cami.

"She's lucid, but keeps fading in and out," she called over the sound of the car crunching through the drifts of snow.

Slowly, Lily's eyes focused and she gasped for air.

"Praise the Lord, I think she's going to make it," Cami said as we neared the hospital.

No sooner had we reached the emergency entrance than a team of doctors rushed out.

"I've got a young lady who's been heavily sedated, a woman suffering from hyperthermia and an injured dog," I said as succinctly as possible.

A moment later, my knees buckled.

"You don't look so good yourself," an emergency nurse said as he grabbed me and hauled me to a gurney.

"Don't worry about me. Help my daughter and Miss Stetson."

I turned and watched a nurse guide Cami to a chair.

"I'm going to get a doctor to look at your leg and your hands and face. That's some pretty bad frostbite," she said.

She looked down at her hands, stiff from the cold. "Yeah, I think you're right. Take care of my dog. His name is Wag, okay?"

The emergency nurse nodded. "He's in good hands. I promise."

Smelling like smoke and suffering from the freezing temperature, I said, "He saved our lives, and I promised I'd take care of him."

The nurse smiled. "It just so happens we have a veterinarian on call. He got caught in the storm and came here to ride it out."

I slid off the gurney and followed the nurse into the emergency room just as he picked up the phone.

"Hey Doc, looks like you've got a patient," he said, giving me a thumbs up.

A minute later, an elderly man wearing a white doctor's smock entered the room. Taking one look at the dog's bloody paws, he smiled. "Let's get him to an examination room where I can get a better look at him."

Once I knew Wag and Cami were in good hands, I made my way to the examination room where a team of doctors worked on Lily. As I drew near, they stepped aside. I took her by the hand. It was warm and soft. A salty tear scalded my cheek. I had come so close to losing her.

Leaning over, I kissed her forehead.

Her eyes cracked open and she mumbled, "Daddy?"

I slid my arms around her and squeezed. "Honey, I thought I'd lost you."

Two slender arms embraced my neck and clung tightly. "It's all so fuzzy, but I do remember. I remember drawing pictures, seeing images, hearing voices."

"Yes, I believe you, Honey. Nate Peterson has been drugging you for a long time, but you rest now. We'll talk about it when you get well."

She relaxed her grip and let her arms fall weakly to her side. "I remember seeing that man. He looked so much like my step-father. I'm just so confused."

"Rest now Lily, you've been through a lot," I said, tucking the covers around her slender body.

"No, I have to tell you so the dreams will go away. He was there. I saw him."

"Who, Honey? Who was there?"

She closed her eyes and waved her hand in a circle as if drawing a picture. "Nelson, Nate's twin brother. He wore a white coat like a cook or waiter. Mr. Sanchez and my mom started arguing at the top of the stairs."

I silenced Lily with an uplifted finger. "I thought Sanchez and Luciano were in the billiard room."

She stared at a distant object. "He must have taken the servant's elevator, but I know he was there. He lunged for the necklace but she pulled back. He lunged again. That's when she lost her footing and stumbled backwards. I tried to stop her from falling but two men grabbed me from behind. It was Nate's brother who slammed into them. By then, it was too late. I watched in horror as mom fell down the stairs." Tears leaked from the corners of her eyes and streamed down the sides of her face.

Carnes statement about a strange man being there smacked me upside the head. What a fool I'd been. I was so focused on finding a link between Luciano and Sanchez, that I totally missed a greater threat ... one that nearly cost me my life.

I knew she had more to tell but didn't want to pressure her. She'd tell me when she was ready.

"He was there all right." Cami's voice interrupted my thoughts.

"Say what?" I cocked my head around. Sitting in a wheelchair, Cami glanced up at me. Her hands were wrapped in bandages, and a large patch of gauze was stretched across her left cheek.

"Dr. Nelson Peterson ... he was there. Like Lily, I too was confused. I saw Nate in the game room watching the game when I took a potty break, but within a minute, a guy passed me carrying an armload of towels. There was something distinctly familiar about his movements, and so I watched him. The first time I saw him, I thought it was Nate, but then I noticed his white service coat. I never gave it another thought until now."

I straightened. "How could that be? He was supposed to be in jail."

"True, but I learned later that he was actually out on bond at the time. He must have sneaked in with the wait staff without a background check. It was Monica who was responsible for him being in jail in the first place. She sued him for malpractice, and he lost. The man was not only consumed with hatred and wanted revenge, but he apparently was infatuated with Lily. When he learned that Monica had milked the governor for a million dollars which, I might add, was put in a trust fund waiting Lily's twenty-first birthday, he got greedy. He must have thought he could pass himself off as his brother, kill Lily and make off with the loot."

I dropped into one of the hospital plastic, formfitting seats, trying to piece it all together. "Yeah, and unfortunately, Lily saw the whole thing."

Lily's chest rose and fell at an even cadence. She looked so peaceful, and my heart yearned to hold her.

"But what about Maurice Rivera and that other man … the one who held Lily back?" Cami asked without thinking.

"That will have to wait. For now, I'm just glad to have my daughter back."

Chapter Forty

It was an unusually mild February day as Cami and I sat at a table in the Indo Cafe on Front Street, along the Sacramento River.

The aroma of fresh pizza mingled with fried onions, and peppers filled the air. A cormorant sat perched on a piling waiting for its next meal, and a couple of children ran ahead of their parents chasing pigeons.

I fingered my glass of half tea, half lemonade and watched Cami finish yet another annoying phone call. It was the third since we'd ordered our meal, and it probably wouldn't be the last.

She shook her head and ended the call. Frustrated, she laid the phone aside. "You were saying?" she asked, trying to restart the conversation.

I blew out a frustrated breath. "I was saying, as I cleaned out the attic of Peterson's house, a pink envelope fell from a shelf. Out of curiosity, I picked it up."

"Did you open it? What did it say?"

I pulled it from my pocket and slid it across the table. "Nope, at first I thought it might have been a letter written to Lily, but it wasn't addressed to her."

Cami lifted it and studied it with interest. "Should we open it?"

A couple of pigeons landed nearby, and I tossed them a crust of bread. The action caused a battle to break out between the two, making me smile.

"Sure, let's see it."

The envelope was completely sealed and tied with a pink string. Like the last guardian of a long-held secret, the string resisted Cami's efforts to untie the knot. Finally, she got it off and with the help of her steak knife, sliced open the seal. Flattening out the single sheet of paper, she flipped it over and held it up for me to see.

My mind raced. What did that picture mean?

It was not the usual stick figures as I'd seen earlier. This was a very detailed picture. It showed a hand shoving Monica backward. Her face was a mask of terror. Just like she said the day we took her to the hospital, but with one distinct difference. In Lily's hand was a golden necklace with a key bearing the letter 'L' at the end.

"What do you think it means?" Cami's question broke the thick silence.

I finished the last bite of my steak before speaking. "It means I've got a long way to go before this is over. Lily will need my protection, understanding and most of all … my love."

The hope of someday asking Cami to marry me seemed further away than ever, but I set that thought aside.

"Look, Cami, I've been thinking about starting my own investigative agency."

Her eyebrows hiked up a notch. "Oh and who would be your first client?"

"I was thinking about reopening Jimmy Barlow's case. Seems the department lost interest in it years ago. Maybe if I solve it, I could get my old job back."

Interest colored Cami's expression. "That's going to cost a lot of money. Who's going to fund it?"

Taking her hand, I gave it a gentle squeeze. "Since Lily doesn't have a place of her own, we have actually been talking about buying a condo. I heard they were converting a warehouse downtown into individual loft units. She mentioned she was interested in buying one of those."

"And what about your agency, is she willing to fund that too?"

"She's as determined to unravel the mystery behind her dreams as I am. And yes, she is willing to put up the money to get me started, on one condition."

Cami finished her tea, wiped her lips, and cocked an eyebrow. "And that condition is …?"

"That I allow her to go to the university and major in criminal justice."

A chuckle bubbled up in Cami's chest. Covering her mouth, she said, "Just like her father. She'll do well … probably better than you, and that's saying something."

I felt a bead of sweat run down the back of my neck.

Eyes narrowing, Cami asked. "What? You don't look too happy with the idea."

"I've not had any practice at parenting, and I'm a bit concerned it won't work out between us. Plus, with me starting an investigative agency, I'll be under a lot of pressure. Do you think you could help out some?"

Her cheeks pinked, and she pushed her chair back. "Trace, there you go again."

My jaw dropped, unable to hide my incredulity. "What?"

"If that is your way of asking me to marry you, forget it."

"No, no, no. I wasn't proposing, I meant if you could help around the office. You know, help me get the filing system setup and all the paperwork done. That's all."

Pulling herself back to the table, she readjusted her napkin. Finger to her chin, she offered me a wry smile. "I have a little comp time. And with Sanchez battling with the press, I could help out for a little while."

Relieved, I leaned back and sighed. "Then that settles it. As soon as Lily is released from the hospital, we'll get to work finding us a place to buy and a storefront to rent. It's going to be interesting the next few months."

Yes it is … very interesting.

Snapshot of a Killer – Book Two
Prologue

It all seemed so simple … in theory.

But then, he didn't live in a theoretical world. His was a world of stark, bloody reality. In his world, there was no room for error. Justice had to be served … raw, unforgiving, painful justice. And he was the one to deliver it.

The problem was … someone knew his plan or at least would as soon as he made his first move.

Killing is indeed, a messy business.

Yes indeed.

But it had to be done.

There are just so many things to think about when one embarks on such an endeavor. Timing, means, and method all had to be planned to the smallest detail. Every possible contingency had to be taken into consideration.

In varying degrees each man on his list had done something to violate his code of justice. Now they had to pay.

He lowered his field glasses, repositioned the ball cap to shade his eyes and made a few notes on a pad. From where he sat in the parking lot, he could see the entire judicial complex. His first target had just left the building and was headed to his car. He noted the man's movements. His routine hadn't changed in weeks and probably wouldn't. *Probably*, that was the operative word.

Once the killing started, there would be no turning back. He knew he was smart, and clever, but was he clever enough? That was the question. He was anxious to find out.

The Chase Newton Series
by Bryan M. Powell

The Order
Follow investigative reporter Chase Newton as he goes undercover in search of the truth. What he finds puts him and those he cares for in mortal danger. Fast-paced and high- energy describes this first of three mystery and action thrillers.

The Oath
The president and vice president have been attacked. The vice president survived, but he is a hunted man. The man who was sworn in is an impostor and Chase must get a DNA from him to prove who the real president is.

The Outsider
After a thousand years of peace, the world is suddenly thrown into chaos as Satan is loosed from his prison. These action-packed stories will hold you breathless and capture your imagination until the exciting conclusion.

The Jared Russell Series
by Bryan M. Powell

Sisters of the Veil
Jared Russell, a former Marine turned architect, must navigate the minefield of hatred and prejudice to find the meaning of love and forgiveness.
ISBN - 978151057994

Power Play - #8 on Amazon Political Fiction
Jared and Fatemah Russell go Beirut, Lebanon, to establish the Harbor House, a refuge for converted Muslims and find themselves caught in a Middle East conflict of global proportions.
ISBN – 9781511402750

The Final Countdown – #25 on Amazon
The clock is ticking and Jared once again finds himself battling against forces beyond his control. Can he and his friends unravel the mystery in time to stop two radical Muslims from perpetrating a horrible crime against our country? ISBN – 978153297825

Non-Fiction Series
by Bryan M. Powell
Seeing Jesus a Three Dimensional Look at Worship

Seeing Jesus is a thought providing and compelling expose' on what is true worship. ISBN -9781511540582

Show Us the Father

A thirty-day devotional showing how Jesus demonstrated His Father's character and qualities. ISBN -9781517633905

Faith, Family, and a Lot of Hard Work

Born the year Stock-Market crashed, Mr. Gillis grew up in South Georgia with a 3rd grade education. After being challenged to get the best job in the company, he worked hard and got a degree from the University of Georgia and Moody Bible Institute in Finance. By mid-life, he owed 14 companies. ISBN -9781467580182

The Witch and the Wise Men

An ancient medallion is discovered,
An evil spirit is awakened,
A witch's curse is broken ... And the wise men of Bethlehem are called upon to face the ultimate evil

The Lost Medallion

Beneath the Hill of Endor is a Temple, Inside the Temple is a Chamber, Inside the Chamber is a door, Behind the door ... the abyss. And the key to the door is the witch's medallion.

The Last Magi

Israel has signed the Peace Accord. The Third Temple is under construction. The world holds its breath as the Ark of the Covenant is rediscovered, and then stolen. It is up to the Magi to find it but then what?

Journey to Edenstrae

What is the Tree of Life survived the Flood and is living in a valley guarded by a Dragon and a warring people?

About the Author

Novelist Bryan M. Powell is a full-time author. Having worked in the ministry for over forty-two years, Bryan is uniquely qualified to write about Christian topics. His novels have been published by Tate Publishing, Lightening Source, Create Space, Kindle Direct Publishing and Vabella Publishing. His novel, The Witch and the Wise Men, held the #23 slot on Amazon's best seller's list and The Lost Medallion hit #22 on Amazon Christian Fantasy.

In addition to his novels, Bryan's short stories and other works appeared in *The North Georgia Writer* (PCWG's publication), *Relief Notes* (A Christian Authors Guild's book, released in 2014), and in the *Georgia Backroads* magazine.

Bryan is a member of the following organizations: American Christian Fiction Writers (ACFW), The Christian Author's Guild (President, 2016), The Paulding County Writers' Guild (PCWG), and the local chapter of ACFW, the New Life Writers Group.

www.facebook.com/authorbryanpowell
www.authorbryanpowell.wordpress.com
authorbryanpowell@gmail.com

Bryan M. Powell

50163468R00133

Made in the USA
Columbia, SC
03 February 2019